Praise for *One Night Tu*

"Shimmering, remarkable. . . . A triumph of a novel, and one that arrives at the perfect time."   **—Michael Schaub, NPR**

"Cooney's warm and hopeful novel is a salve for these times."
—Juliana Rose Pignataro, *Newsweek*

"Wise and warm. . . . This is a quiet book, steady, gentle, present, one that grapples with the matter-of-fact here and now, and wades, with bravery and wonder, into the mysteries that make us human."
—Nina MacLaughlin, *The Boston Globe*

"The perfect novel to combat pandemic angst."
—*Kirkus,* **starred review**

"Cooney's novel expands the concept of what's possible, imagining hope where there is none and pointing always toward the light."
—Mari Carlson, *BookPage,* **starred review**

"Takes place over the course of a night shift at an urban medical center whose cavernous immensity—'steel and glass and stone, lights muted in the deep surround of the dark'—gives it the feel of a modern-day cathedral. . . . The word 'soul' is a frequent presence in this novel, a kind of familiar spirit."
—Sam Sacks, *The Wall Street Journal*

"Now, more than ever, we need to be reminded that hope prevails—and this novel does exactly that."

—**Carolyn Quimby,** *The Millions*

"A poetic story of wandering souls, filled with the beauty of human encounters and the sorrows of departure."   —**Dorthe Nors**

"Whenever I read Ellen Cooney, I feel like I am in the presence of a cunning medium—an unwavering mind reader of memories, dreams. *One Night Two Souls Went Walking* has the familiarity of old fairy-tale books, the steadiness of Tove Jansson, the abstraction of Silvina Ocampo, and something entirely new. A lovely and grave novel."   —**Kate Bernheimer**

"It's the very rare book that pierces both spirit and sense of humor. *One Night Two Souls Went Walking* wrapped me in its warm wisdom from the start. Reading it was like reading a Mary Oliver poem or Marilynne Robinson novel—radiant, humane, splendidly joyous."   —**Alyson Hagy**

Praise for Ellen Cooney

"This remarkably talented author writes in a refined, understated prose."   —*New York Times*

"A writer with style and heart."   —*O, The Oprah Magazine*

"Ellen Cooney has a talent for creating fine, quirky characters."
     —*Washington Post*

"Cooney writes with light grace."   —*Boston Globe*

A Cowardly

Woman No More

Also by Ellen Cooney

A Cowardly
Woman No More

A Novel

Ellen Cooney

COFFEE HOUSE PRESS
Minneapolis
2023

Coffee House Press books are available to the trade through our primary distributor, Consortium Book Sales & Distribution, cbsd.com or (800) 283-3572. For personal orders, catalogs, or other information, write to info@coffeehousepress.org.

Coffee House Press is a nonprofit literary publishing house. Support from private foundations, corporate giving programs, government programs, and generous individuals helps make the publication of our books possible. We gratefully acknowledge their support in detail in the back of this book.

LIBRARY OF CONGRESS CATALOGING-IN-PUBLICATION DATA

Names: Cooney, Ellen, author.
Title: A cowardly woman no more / Ellen Cooney.
Description: Minneapolis : Coffee House Press, 2023.
Identifiers: LCCN 2022037391 (print) | LCCN 2022037392 (ebook) |
     ISBN 9781566896719 (paperback) | ISBN 9781566896726 (epub)
Classification: LCC PS3553.O5788 C69 2023 (print) |
     LCC PS3553.O5788 (ebook) | DDC 813/.54—dc22
LC record available at https://lccn.loc.gov/2022037391
LC ebook record available at https://lccn.loc.gov/2022037392

PRINTED IN THE UNITED STATES OF AMERICA
30 29 28 27 26 25 24 23   1 2 3 4 5 6 7 8

*To Michael Cooney, who's been listening
to his mom read her words for his entire life.*

A Cowardly
Woman No More

One

The Rose & Emerald was back from the dead, and they said it was a comet, as if a mighty, long-tail ball of rocks and ice and gas came rushing through space one winter night, aiming for them like a bomb.

At last things were normal again in the lane with no other addresses, in the middle of a valley in the middle of Massachusetts. No tarps to cover damages. No small army of hardhats, plumbers, hammerers, painters. No Temporarily Closed as an overlay on their big wooden sign, high up on rustic fence posts, where the country lane rolled away from the old main road.

The sign was repainted often, but never changed: a single red rose, long stemmed, leafy, without thorns, on a background of shiny green as emerald as green can be.

Only that. They were famous. They didn't need words to say their name.

The building had been there a long time: a sprawling wood frame, white clapboards, pale gray shutters, old oak doors, stone chimneys, and a checkerboard of a roof, with slate tiles the colors of clay. Overall, it looked like a stately country mansion that was also unfussy and earthy, like a tavern that's mostly genteel, but always ready to host a brawl.

Around the building were sugar maples, willows, birches, holly bushes, and little glens of fragrant juniper. There were lawns of soft grass, and long-ago farmland they had turned into meadows, carefully mowed with footpaths for strolling.

Across the main road, beyond mossy, crumbling stone walls, a wild-looking orchard was full of staunch, gnarly trees so fierce in expression, they looked like they would bite you if you went in there and tried to prune them.

Out back of the building, past the meadows, a woodlot of just a few acres could give the impression it was a deep, dark forest, stretching miles and miles, like it belonged to the world of a myth.

And off in the distance, past those trees, was the mountain called Wachusett—but it was more of a giant hill than an actual mountain. It stood alone on the flat horizon, like a dinosaur, gorgeous out the windows of the Rose & Emerald banquet hall, either sunlit or moonlit or in smoky shadows of clouds: a solitary brontosaurus out there grazing, with a hump smoothly rounded, and the tail, neck, and head out of view.

"Well, we had this comet that came over the hill."

The Rose & Emerald would not give up on their story. They didn't care that no one believed them.

Of everyone working as staffers, and everyone involved in the repairs, no one stepped forward to blame the Temporarily Closed on a normal catastrophe. There were plenty to choose from. A furnace that should have been replaced a long time ago was kept working until it exploded. A tower of a sick old tree had fallen on them in a terrible crash. The foundation sill had finally caved, and collapsed into sawdust, or pipes froze and burst, or a weight-bearing beam could not bear weight another minute, and cracked and broke and gave up.

It could have been anything. They would never admit the truth of their existence: they cared more about their appearance than the needs of their inner realities.

They had no social media accounts. Their internet presence was a website offering basic information and scenic photos in all the seasons.

But the tale of the comet spread widely. Late one night in January, during an icy, windy snowstorm, when all the telescopes in the world were off, or pointed in other directions, and all the satellites in orbit missed it too, the comet tore down in a breathtaking arc and attacked them, leaving no evidence.

They claimed it was pulverized at impact. No one was injured. They had hosted a large fundraising event that evening for a local politician, but ended it early, thanks to weather reports of the oncoming blizzard. They shut the whole place down before nine. No one lived on the premises, or anywhere closely nearby.

Their surveillance cameras were really just for show. Anyway their cameras had been destroyed.

Did that mean they had no witnesses?

No, it did not. Of course they had witnesses, or how would they know what hit them? Unfortunately, the people who saw the comet were shy, and valued their privacy, and wished to be anonymous to the outside world.

Now it was June.

The day was a Wednesday. The time was a little before eleven, too early for opening the bar, the patio café, and the public dining rooms. A convoy of shuttle buses pulled into the parking lot at the start of the lane. When the dust settled, because nothing around here was paved, one hundred eighty-two people stepped onto the grounds of the Rose & Emerald, and formed a scattered procession down the lane to the entrance of the banquet hall.

Well here we are!

Two

Our company's annual banquet and awards ceremony was about to begin. Nothing looked different due to the shutdown, but everything was fixed up and shiny.

The day was soft and summery, the light golden yellow like a halo. All the greenery looked freshly washed. Out in the meadows, bright, vivid wildflowers were almost pulsing on their stems with aliveness. Wachusett was perfectly clear, against a sky that could not be bluer.

We had traveled from the concrete mini-city of our office park, fronted by a major highway, backed by a slightly lesser one. No matter how anyone felt about this event, or the company we worked for, it was easy to accept a few moments of serenity, just from the pleasure of arriving.

I was on the last bus, among the last to disembark. Trisha Donahue is my name. It was Trisha Gilley before I married.

On the bus, I found myself among people I didn't know, from departments nowhere near mine. I could have gone to the trouble of joining conversations or even introducing myself, like I was interested in being sociable and making new friends.

But I was all right with keeping quiet.

The entrance to the banquet hall was from a side porch the Rose & Emerald liked to call a New England veranda, although it was narrow, and the benches were low, and only decorative, like colonial antiques in a museum. I had to step carefully on the crushed-rock path. I wasn't used to wearing heels. When I paused and looked around, I tried to make it seem I was reveling in the views, not worrying about my balance. I'd bought the shoes online and hadn't realized, when I ordered them, how spiky they'd be. I'd planned to send them back, but never got around to it.

I stayed upright. I didn't wobble at all. I was doing fine. I nodded in agreement when I heard someone up ahead pleasantly humming the tune of "Oh, What a Beautiful Mornin'." It sounded quite nice, and I was almost willing to believe the day ahead would not be awful for me.

But soon I'd be wondering why no one in my department told me I'd been chosen Employee of the Year.

No cash prize was awarded with the honor. Not that any amount of money would have made it all right.

Officially, the identity of the winner was meant to be kept a secret. Only your own department knew. Your administrator or manager, and your closest workmates, had the job of coming up with stories of you, and photos of you to be flashed on a mega-large screen.

The company's different sections functioned on an everyday basis like islands in one area of an ocean. In my eight years there, in the reality of how many minutes are in a day, I never squeezed in the simple thing of making friends outside my own turf. Banquet Day was the one time we were all thrown together.

Entering the vestibule by Big Hall, as the banquet room was called, you came to a glass bowl, like a fishbowl, on a stand that would otherwise hold a vase of flowers or a guest book. In the bowl were numbers on folded bits of paper, corresponding to seats at the tables. You picked a number and headed for your chair. That was the seating plan. There was no head table.

The executive whose office took charge of the banquet had sent out a memo reminding us about mingling and connecting, especially with fellow employees who were strangers. My department believed in going renegade. We weren't a large unit—we took up one table altogether. We would grab a number from the bowl and muscle ourselves into swaps, so we could stick together and still be islanders. Every year it was this way.

I thought they were my friends. Not friends like actual friends you have all sorts of ties to, all sorts of history and complications. Work friends. I never saw any of them outside the company. As far as I knew, they didn't invite each other to their homes, or go out socializing as a group.

Work friends should count as something that matters, I had believed.

Some past winners of the biggest prize had not been caught off guard. The last two had taken an acceptance speech from a jacket pocket. I'd heard that the man who won last year was allowed to treat the presentation like a Facebook profile, overseeing everything himself for the ten minutes or so when Employee of the Year was the star of the show.

I realized it was supposed to be a big deal that I was the first woman. But that only made it worse.

Why didn't anyone on my team give me a heads-up? Instead I was stunned by the wrongness, and I was suddenly sitting in a spotlight, because of course at the Rose & Emerald they had one. It came rushing across the hall, aiming only for me, and it was blazingly, blindingly white.

Three

The calming quiet lay everywhere, joining smells of newly mown grass and cooking. The kitchen windows were open to their screens. The closer you went, the more you came in contact with previews of what you'd be eating.

Not everyone looked forward to the meal. Some in the company called the food offensive, in terms of being heavy and artless. And even boring.

Offensive and heavy and artless!

And even boring!

Those words had been uttered at the highest levels of the company—uttered and repeated and leaked.

The banquet offerings weren't drawn from the regular menus. They were the same every year. The office handling Banquet Day had instructed us to make our choices via an online form specially created and sent out. I had not done so.

There were no appetizers or soups. You went straight to the plates.

The entrée list had pot roast from an old-time cookbook; roasted turkey, like Thanksgiving, either white or dark or both, with or without stuffing; boneless, breaded baked chicken so crispy it seemed fried; a dense and creamy chicken or turkey pot pie with savory seasonings and no vegetables, and if you wanted to go vegetarian, four-cheese baked macaroni many people enjoyed eating with spoons. You could also order the mac and cheese as a side.

And there were potatoes from a roast, or mashed with lots of cheddar; buttery and garlicky green beans; spinach creamed instead of steamed or sautéed; creamed corn; baked squash that was marinated in maple syrup, and tender circles of onions fried in the secret Rose & Emerald batter, which was based very amply on beer.

And creamy Caesar salads, pitchers of gravy, silver tubs of cranberry sauce, baskets of cornbread and rolls.

Then would come buffets of layer cakes, pies, fudgy brownies, bread pudding, bowls of whipped cream, and minimal offerings of fruit, even if fruit was requested ahead of time, as if "fresh fruit for dessert" meant bananas in the banana creams, lemon zest in the lemon cakes with lemony cream cheese frosting, brown-sugared apples in pies where the crust rose high above the plates in golden domes of, it was said, it was leaked, way too much pastry.

After last year's banquet, everyone became aware that an upscale hotel, palatial in size, would be constructed within walking distance of the office park. Exciting things were promised: first-class amenities, chefs with culinary degrees and awards, views from the function rooms of the Boston skyline, shimmery in the distance to the south, like a mirage.

With such a dark cloud looming, many employees, in fact a clear majority, took to an internal message board where you could post without names. I wasn't one of them. But I was happy to see my opinions expressed.

Switch the location for banquets? No way!

Keep the tradition alive where it fucking belongs!

The Rose & Emerald RULES!

Fuck all snobs forever!

There were delays with the new hotel. So far, nothing was going on except trucking in heaps of dirt, so the hotel could stand on a hill. That was why we were here again this year. We knew that in spite of all protests, our opposition was futile. The switch was destined to happen.

The feeling of doom among the majority wasn't quite at the level of gloom—not today, not when the day was so fine. But you had to factor it in.

So what if they didn't give corporate discounts, and the place was out of the way? And you had to put up with things that could seem a little too much?

A few on the waitstaff had been here so long, and were so old, you could hold your breath in anxiety, fearing your server might have a heart attack or a stroke; you might choose to risk making a scene by jumping up to relieve them of a heavy tray. The tables were oak, like the doors. Some had wobbly or uneven legs, propped at the feet by plywood squares that did not seem up to the job of lending support. The chairs, also oak, also old, were not cushioned. Tall people had to watch out for low doorways. The white linen tablecloths were threadbare here and there, and gave off, before the food arrived, a faint but annoying aroma of bleach. In the bathrooms, the sinks looked as old as the building. The old-fashioned roller towels were always getting jammed. If you didn't know which toilets were modernized and which weren't, you could find yourself working the flush with the pull chain dangling above, like something weird had happened to time, and you'd fallen out of your own century.

You might wonder if things could happen to you in this place that never happened before. Maybe you would find that alarming, but maybe not.

Four

I felt at home here.

I was intimate with the Rose & Emerald. Unlike my colleagues, I grew up in the valley. But not in this exact area. On the main road, and along the many lanes, houses were new and upscale, and wildly expensive.

I was a local among transplants: the only child of parents who spent their whole working lives in a now-disappeared tool-and-die shop that was once a dairy processing plant. My father was on the maintenance crew. My mother, a part-timer, worked as a roving packer, moving around from one conveyor belt to another when a regular packer went on a break, or when extra hands were needed because a belt was switched to a faster speed, then faster, faster.

Sometimes they brought home assortments of small objects, as a stamp collector would gather stamps. Manufacturing in America could not, absolutely could not, happen without these things, I learned young. The machines in their shop made components for other machines. Yet I was not allowed to ask what the various pieces were for, or what they were called, or which other pieces they were meant to fit into. I'd get a scolding. They would complain about me, wondering, why did I ask questions they had no answers for?

I never found out what happened to the carton filled with their collection. Like so much else, it was there in our lives one day, and not the next.

The workers' rowhouses where my home used to be were all gone, all razed. My parents liked to joke that their dream of old-age life somewhere in Florida had come true, because they moved to a retirement village thirty miles to the south, as if "going any-where even a little bit south" had been the dream. They liked to say that if you stayed indoors with the heat cranked up for part of every year, you could imagine there was no such thing as winter.

They felt they had landed in luxury. Those rowhouses were flimsy and cramped and cold.

The distance from home to the Rose & Emerald was a little under three miles, which was nothing to me as a child, once I had a bike. The Rose & Emerald was where I ventured, often on my own, regularly, freely, fearlessly, although sometimes when I was pedaling hard in the dark, alone on long stretches with no street-lights, I became a little nervous.

I'd leave the bike by a tree and hike around like I lived here. Like it was a residence and I was one of the gentry, not one of the help.

I was happy here. I pestered kitchen people for handouts and glasses of water. I looked into windows, loving the sight of my breath fogging up the glass, like I was leaving my mark, even though my tiny, flat clouds evaporated so quickly.

I trick-or-treated at their front door. On my last Halloween, when I felt I wasn't too old yet, I sneaked out dressed as a rob-ber, in a black wool hat, an eye mask that was also black, and a cardboard sign on my chest, dangling on a loop of string, say-ing in black Magic Marker, the letters balloony and filled in, "ROBBER." I dared to go into the bar for money instead of candy. In one hand I had a grocery bag, in the other a water pistol I happened to find one day on the sidewalk in front of a stand-alone house with a backyard pool. I knew the girl who lived there, but I was never invited to come over in my swimsuit, or invited there at all.

I quickly ran out of water to squirt at bar customers. But when my adventure came to an end, I left the Rose & Emerald with enough cash to fix up my bike. It had come to me from my parents, who brought it home one day from work. Their shop held events now and then called "swap meets." Which was a way to not say "charity donations you can go into a room and take." Probably quite a few girls had owned my bike before I did.

Thanks to that night, I had the chain replaced. I bought a new seat so I could finally throw out the tattered old one. And when my cash ran out, the kindly elderly guy at the bike shop, who looked a little like Santa Claus, gave me a free, snazzy headlight, and reflectors too. Then I didn't have to be afraid any longer of the dark.

Soon afterward, I became part of a girl gang who came from rowhouses too. Or, in general, from that place we would hear about, always in a certain tone of voice—the place that classmates of ours loved to refer to as *the wrong side of the tracks.*

We'd taunt them right back, while knowing precisely what they meant. What tracks? There's no train through here! There's no tracks, you dumb-ass, piss-face, walking-and-talking pieces of shit!

With my gang, I loved heading for the Rose & Emerald best when it was apple season. We hid our bikes in the juniper, and crossed the main road to sneak into the orchard. There used to be a little shack where employees handled customers. There were often days set aside for pick-your-own; it could get crowded. We'd go far into the rear, where no one else went except deer and birds and squirrels and woodchucks. There, we scavenged for windfalls, stole off the trees, and screamed with joy when we played snowball fights with soft, rotting apples.

My prom was held at the Rose & Emerald. I didn't go, but I went there all the same, keeping out of sight, feeling proud of myself for not joining in.

I got drunk for the first time very late one night while sitting around with my gang on the patio like we were paying customers.

I peed and threw up in the Rose & Emerald meadows.

Before I had sex for real, I blissfully pleased myself while imagining I was out in the forest at night, on a soft, dry bed of moss, listening to breezes stirring leaves, and to birds who speak only in the dark. Sometimes an imaginary boyfriend was involved. Sometimes I had the sense I was better off on my own.

In my second year of college, when I was home on a break, some of my old friends invited me to take part in a weekend activity: dressing up and gate-crashing Rose & Emerald events, where they could blend in before the real guests settled down to dinner. They enjoyed snagging appetizers, cruising around, and making visits to an open bar, as many as possible.

I couldn't take part. I was already too different. I had set my sights elsewhere.

Later, I would have held my wedding here, in a completely secular way. But the family of my husband-to-be started turning up the pressure to pick their church, followed by a reception in a restaurant they were patrons of. "Swank" was not the name of this particular place, but that was the word I used in thinking about it. The rental cost of the function room alone was equal to one month of the salary I'd been earning.

My husband-to-be took my side, having left all the planning to me. Small and low-key, I had thought: a ceremony in a meadow, a small lunch on the patio, and keep the expenses low. Doing it my own way, I had thought. I had no savings. My parents could only help a little.

Then up spoke his, with an offer to write the checks for everything. They assured me that if I chose the Rose & Emerald, they would do their best to understand why.

I did not see a way to say no.

I was being practical.

I was making necessary decisions.

But sometimes, in the early years of my marriage, I wished I'd stuck up for myself about wanting to take a drive here for photos in my white silk cloud of a gown, with the mountain behind me, and the woods, and the wildflowers all around. I was also being practical when I decided to keep quiet about it. To hold myself back from saying, "I want."

I wasn't the one paying the photographer. I would have caused trouble. I would have been a spoiler. Everything about that day had been carefully, exquisitely orchestrated, right down to every second.

Practical. Maybe that was another way of saying, "I lost my old nerve."

Or, "I adapted."

Or, "I turned corporate."

Five

The banquet used to begin around one, and come to a finish whenever it was done, like a baseball game. Once or twice it whizzed by like an almost no-hitter, and everyone walked out more or less sober. But mostly we had extra, boozy innings. That was the original reason for chartering buses.

The days of calling Banquet Day a party day were over. In the last few years the company had grown sleek and even stern, turning traitor in many ways to its scruffy, adventurous, friendly old self. Management had changed. The founders, who'd be mortified if you called them executives, were all gone.

Now for Banquet Day, we had a slightly shorter version of a workday, starting from gathering in the office park where the buses waited.

It was all plotted out and measured: travel time, meal, presentations, coffee break with maybe a second round of desserts. Before boarding your bus for the trip back to the office park, you had the option of a stroll on the grounds, which could also include taking photos and making videos. The company urged you to send these to the marketing and public-image people. There were contests for the best submissions, but I never heard of any promised prizes given out.

Attending the banquet wasn't mandatory, according to the company. But it wasn't exactly optional.

You could take it as a vacation day. They kept lists of who attended and who didn't. If you failed to declare your day off ahead of time, like you thought you'd get away with playing truant, you would still receive a memo explaining that your next paycheck would be normal, but your next vacation week would be docked by one day. Quite a few people took the docking. I knew that some employees slipped out after eating, having arranged for someone to pick them up. Some would call Uber or Lyft. I suspected there was a list of the sneak-outers too.

I almost didn't go. The night before, I did not lay out an outfit. The company now had a banquet dress code, same as if going to a wedding.

The speeches could go on and on, heading into what felt like a forever, and so did the rituals, promotional videos, descriptions of goals accomplished, outlooks for the future, displays of charts, a slideshow of employee photos, then another, of last year's banquet.

The CEO delivered his keynote while strolling among the tables, mic in hand, ad-libbing like he was running a rally he didn't need prepared remarks for, and if you didn't look up at him when he paused in your area, he'd come over and stand close to you until you did. Managers got up on their feet to tell jokes about people in their departments. Sometimes the jokes could be funny, unless you were the one they made fun of. Sometimes the skittering laughter was tinny, unreal.

It was hard to keep up an expression of having a good time, but a photographer and a videographer would be there. Photos and clips would soon appear on the company's website and in their social feeds. You never knew when you'd be on camera.

You were required to turn off your phone and keep it out of reach.

Liquor was no longer allowed. You couldn't even order a beer. The sliding door in the corridor between the banquet hall and the bar was closed. The bar opened at noon, but it was off-limits unless you went outdoors and walked around the building to the front, which took a long time, and anyway the bar was popular. It was always crowded around lunch time.

But still. Not go to the banquet! I had given up hoping the old ways would return, but I'd never missed one before.

Absolutely, I meant to stay home. I rarely had the house to myself. I looked forward to the luxury of peaceful aloneness. But at the last minute, I changed my mind, with barely enough time to shower, grab something to wear, and make it to the buses. I didn't want my name on the list of truants. I didn't want to look like I was holding such a grudge, I was making a statement by my absence.

By the time Banquet Day arrived, I had known for a week that the company passed me over for the promotion I expected so deeply, I felt it was mine already. Every passing day of that week made me feel a little worse. I hadn't even told my husband.

I wasn't trying to keep a secret. I had the sense I should worry about my brain. It kept randomly clogging up, and then all I could think about was how hard it was to think. My entire inside-self kept switching its inner settings to Mute, Delete, No Service Available.

I was helpless to help myself. I was in shock. I was trying my best to say it was no big deal, but I couldn't even find a way to lie to myself.

It kept on being, *I can't believe this. I just can't.*

Six

A promotion was going to happen.

Back before the new regime, I was comfortable with the company's bosses—the founders. They had structured the company without the ranks that were now in place. But the track I entered at my hiring turned out to be a loop I was stuck in, going nowhere but around and around.

Not that I was hired in an ordinary way.

I had been recruited.

"But I'm lucky," I used to say to myself.

I was very aware of what I had. My salary was too high to find fault with. My cost-of-living raises were big enough to notice. My benefits package was much, much better than at the two other companies where I'd been. My commute was easy. I could avoid the highways and drive through a quiet, well-kept suburb of houses spaced widely apart, which looked a lot like the one where I lived.

I knew it could be risky with the company to take a maternity leave. You might return to find they'd kept their promise to take you back and not demote you, but you'd see right away you'd been diminished, in ways large or small. Or you might be denied any sort of advancement, like you'd bailed on them, and you'd never be able to make up for it. But I was post-babies. At the time of my recruitment, my first was in day care, my second in preschool. Two sons. Now they were twelve and ten.

My manager wasn't a parent, but he cut me slack when I left for school events or to handle some crisis. When I stayed home with a sick child, I could work remotely. On snow days, when everything shut down except work, I didn't have to go in.

I couldn't prove this, but I felt there was some underlying resentment toward me, never voiced, never rising to the level of words. It was a background static that came and went randomly. The dads in my department weren't offered the perks that came my way, not that I asked for them. But then, every time a dad went on leave for a new baby, he returned to pick up where he'd left off. It was, welcome back, no hard feelings, no repercussions, like he'd taken a vacation.

My department used to be larger, with our own administrative assistant. In the cutbacks taking place when the new regime began, the young woman in that job was labeled nonessential. We now shared an older, higher-level administrator with another section. This woman was somewhat of an extra member of our team, appearing and disappearing. She could be ghostly to us. Her primary allegiances were in the other section.

That made me the one woman in mine.

But I never thought of it that way. I never went around thinking, oh, look at this, I'm the only woman.

I could talk myself into believing that nothing mattered except being professional and also very good at what you do.

I liked my job more than I didn't. I wasn't bored as a regular part of my day, reaching the end all dull and empty, and exhausted from the effort of fighting off being bored. It was only now and then.

In the company where I worked before this one, I'd become scared. It was a killer sort of fright, like my brain was in danger, because my work was so easy it was tranquilizing me. The most frightening part was that I'd started to like it that way. I saw I could be good at being lazy, and no one would ever know. And then the rest of my work life might proceed in that manner, with me taking things easy, just coasting along, while at the same time making more money. And saying to myself, "This is such a perfect way to have a job!"

In my department, I appreciated the free, catered, excellent trays of appetizers and sandwiches at our weekly lunches. Our coffee was good. The espresso machine worked more often than it was broken. I only needed to go now and then to the office park Starbucks.

Within the office park, there was a network of flat, smooth sidewalks. The company offered a discount membership to the gym in the building next to mine, but I couldn't spare the time. I went outside for twenty minutes or half an hour middays, in almost all weather, walking around and around, sometimes extremely rapidly. I ate lunch most days at my desk. I kept rain gear and a hoodie or jacket in my car, and snow boots in winter. If I worked up too much of a sweat, I always had a change of shirts folded up in my briefcase, and deodorant in my handbag.

I was glad for the casualness of wearing jeans and sneakers whenever I felt like jeans and sneakers.

My evaluations were documents bearing witness to *excellence in knowledge and delivery; an expert-level skill set; reports and memos notable for consistent clarity; no outstanding weakness to be addressed.*

I could take what they called a "personal day" up to six times a year. That didn't include sick days, which were officially unlimited.

My vacation time was up to four weeks. I didn't protest the new rule where I had to agree to take my weeks one by one, spread out evenly in the seasons. And I was now required to submit my chosen weeks in a schedule I had to prepare well ahead. A vacation calendar was part of my statement at the start of the year, of my work goals and the new things I planned to learn. It was understood that I could be called while away if something came up. When they called me, pretty much every vacation, I told myself it was all right.

I could see that I should feel I was important. I would wonder why I didn't.

Last year in March I needed to check the statement; my annual review was coming up. I discovered the wrong dates for July. The Fourth was on a Friday. I was already looking forward to having my holiday begin as I drove away from work on the Thursday.

It seemed I had mistakenly put down the last week of the month as the one I wanted.

I could not believe what a hassle it was to get approval for the correction. Did the company have a new policy of trying to make you feel that the stakes were so high in your job, it could happen that, if you made a mistake of any kind, someone, somewhere, as a result, might be harmed, might even die?

Yet nothing was a life-or-death emergency. I was an analyst. I did things with software. I programmed sometimes, if I had to. I wrote reports. I studied problems. I put forth conclusions, solutions, opinions, forecasts, recommendations. My materials were facts, figures, data. I went into a cubicle to do my job, not to the site of some disaster, or out on a rescue mission in a dangerous place.

Make a change in March for a vacation four months away? Was I aware of the trouble that would cause? But, on the other hand, seeing how it said in black and white that I had claimed the last week of July, would I consider keeping it that way, since so many other employees took off time around the Fourth?

I had tried to imagine what I'd do if my request for the correction was turned down.

Which it wasn't. Then I felt weird in a creepy way for suspecting I had not made an error. That I did my calendar right, same as always, and after I turned it in, it was changed.

It was all just stupid protocol stuff, I decided. When you work at a job, you put up with things.

Whenever the thought crossed my mind that I could leave the company, I was quick to shut it down.

No other companies in the office park had any sort of job I could apply for. I'd have a much longer commute no matter where I went. The only places in fairly easy driving distance were the two companies I'd left.

I could not afford any extra minutes of drive time.

Not with my schedule as it was.

In my family we had good routines. We were settled. The boys were deeply rooted in their school, which was a feeder to the academy they took for granted would be their high school. Every dollar of what that school cost us was completely, unquestionably worth it. I reminded myself of that all the time, like a fact that needed testing, and always remained a hard fact.

My husband graduated from the academy. So had his parents and his two sisters. My children would be free to consider other high schools, but they most probably wouldn't. They'd been going to events at the academy since they were babies bundled in strollers: soccer, homecomings, fundraisers, holiday gatherings, basketball, baseball, all sorts of events. I did my best to participate. Sometimes at a game I'd be sitting with my family in the bleachers, at work on my laptop or iPad, while feeling truly, ridiculously happy because my three guys were yelling and cheering and having a great time.

My family.

We were safe. We were secure. All of us together were solid.

Moving away from our home, I'd felt, was out of the question. The thought of getting my family to relocate for a job for me would be the same as if I'd helmed the *Titanic,* as if I'd stood at the steering wheel and said to myself, "Okay, I'm taking us into that iceberg."

And I was the one who picked our suburb! I was the one who fell in love with our house, sitting in its quiet, sheltered half circle: six houses altogether, positioned like numbers on the top half of a clock, nine to three.

Ours was at ten, a modern colonial like the others, two and a half stories, or three and a half if you included the finished basement.

The structure was high in the ceilings, widely roomy in all the rooms.

There was a driveway, gently sloped, paved, and resealed or repaved whenever the slightest defect occurred.

A double garage with a loft.

A back deck with a retractable roof, same as a convertible's.

A backyard big enough for another house lot, not that the zoning permitted it.

A front lawn where weeds were not allowed to grow, where parching in the summer was not allowed to happen.

Outdoor lights on sensors, not glaring like at some of the other houses, but as cozy and soft as candlelight.

Privet hedges, weeping willows, a red oak, boxwood shrubs, flower beds, all taken care of, along with the lawns, by the landscaping people, as floor-washing and vacuuming and the bathrooms and window-washing were left to the cleaners who came in once a week, but it never felt often enough.

Home.

And everything I'd wanted. Everything I used to believe I'd never have.

When my husband and I took out our mortgage, I was loaded with college loans, and they were a long way from being paid off. His parents had given us a generous gift of money—not a loan—to cover the down payment. I had thought we should rent for a while. I had pictured a small apartment, easy to take care of, no big expenses.

But, investments! I needed to start being someone who thought about investments!

I'd known plenty of people in college and grad school with no personal concept of what it's like to worry about money for basic stuff you needed. My husband took it to a whole new level. He rarely gave a thought to what anything cost. If he looked at a price tag at all, it was only because I made him.

But he agreed with me that after we accepted the house money, we would stand on our own feet and be independent. We would draw the line about taking money from his family. I sometimes wondered if they slipped him cash, or funneled money to him some other way, without my knowing. I never asked.

The mortgage on our house was very large. I never said out loud that we should have waited several years before taking on that kind of debt.

I would wonder, and never mention it, how are we going to keep up payments on everything we have to keep paying?

Yet I knew I was lucky.

I would think of the globe. I would think of Earth, not as a marble of a planet in space, but as a round container holding figures of people, where many, many, many more people have it bad than have it good. That was how I put it to myself: stark and simple. That was what it came down to.

I moved up, way up, and now I have it so, so good.

I never talked about this at work, but I was a woman who went home every day to a table already set and waiting, and dinner either ready or cooking. On my drive home, I could transform myself into a blankness, like a resting point, suspended between the Trisha who was the Trisha at work and the Trisha who was the wife and the mom, lucky, lucky, lucky.

My husband's company was located close to home, like mine, but in a different direction. He had clients and colleagues in parts of the world with wildly different time zones from us. He started his workdays much earlier than I did. At his last yearly review, he was given the chance to change his hours, but he wouldn't even consider it. He was home by midafternoon.

I never said a thing about knowing that the three of them spent much of their time together playing video games, and not the educational ones I was always buying. I pretended that the house I came home to wasn't throbbing with leftover vibrations from digital fights, and blowing things up, and walking along a sidewalk with an ax, in case you needed to swing it at someone's head, and soccer games where it wasn't a penalty if you could score by making the other team's goalie blind, deaf, legless, and armless, by magic. Or you could have the power, if you earned it, to just approach the goalie and vaporize him.

Mom's home!

Like they'd only been doing something civilized. I would force myself not to think about the mess in the kitchen from food preparation and cooking; the wrangling ahead over homework and bedtime; the husband wanting alone time with me, but he had to be asleep by nine because he had to wake up at four thirty; the online class I was taking as part of learning new things, and it couldn't be done during work time; the emails and texts and voice mails I had to plow through about things like appointments and field trips and neighborhood get-togethers and whatever was going on with my parents and parents-in-law too, since I was the one who did most of the communicating with my husband's family, which everyone seemed to feel was required of me. And then piles of laundry that had to be done because everyone was out of clean underwear, and mail in the mail basket that piled up too, and most of it was junk but had to be taken care of, and hair removal I needed to do, so I never went to work with even a shadow of a lady's mustache, and I never had the time or the patience in the morning.

I didn't dare take sleeping pills, out of fear I'd wake too groggily. Sometimes, before falling asleep, I believed that sleep would never come. My husband would wake sometimes when I reached for him, and even when fucking was quick and matter of fact, we both loved it. We loved coming dramatically, intensely, while muffling our voices into each other's skin.

We still had that.

And even when we weren't really into it and just went through the motions, exhausted as we'd be, we still could turn it around into a very fine time.

"Thank God this never gets old," he'd mumble.

And I would lie beside him and wonder what he was dreaming, and what the kids were dreaming too, as if I'd never again have dreams of my own. I would toss and turn and do my best to stop myself from going over in my head all the dumb things I did that day, and all the words I spoke, and wrote, that should have been other, better words, and all the errors that might or might not exist in whatever report I'd filed with the company, which I might not have proofread carefully. On and on these things could go. Yet none were based on actual data, actual facts, in terms of what went on in my daily work life.

It was like having delusions of grandeur, except delusions of being totally incompetent. I would bundle my pillow around my head like I could silence the noise of my own mind.

But all along, every evening, I walked through the door of home to four places set at the table. There would be salad in the big wooden bowl, as if I weren't the only one who'd eat salad. And creamed spinach, almost as good as the Rose & Emerald's, and steam in the air from water at a boil for spaghetti, or the sizzle and smell of burgers, or all the stuff laid out for tacos. Or pizza, or Chinese food, delivered five minutes ago, and how many women in the world walk into their kitchen and all they have to do about dinner is sit down and eat it?

I would remember all over again how good I had it.

And I'd cheer up, or calm down, like an itch that doesn't itch because you scratched it. Like the itch will never come back.

I am so lucky.

Seven

I never went to HR or my manager with a problem. Complaints of any kind went into your file.

My manager was fairly new to the company. I waited until he settled in before I spoke to him about my career. We went over my history, including the memo from the headhunters responsible for bringing me in, back in the old days.

It turned out that while I was panicky-scared in my second company, when I was so frightened of losing myself in the boredom of a job too easy for me, I was being spied on by I never knew who. Someone in my department had a side gig as a spotter for the recruiting place. I received an email inviting me to talk about my future. Which I ignored like any piece of spam.

But they kept at it until I finally gave them my phone number and said I was open to a meeting.

"We saw her potential and seized her," the memo said.

My manager felt that recruiters were robbers breaking into other businesses. He used to be a headhunter himself. He complimented me for being a woman worthy of stealing.

I thought the meeting went well.

But nothing resulted. I was wary about pressing the issue of a better position. I knew what could happen if you called the wrong attention to yourself. You might be watched a little too closely, a little too negatively. A next evaluation could be lower. A few words might be said about weaknesses suddenly in need of fixing.

Meanwhile, into the company came new hires: kids who called me "ma'am" or "Mrs. Donahue." They dropped cheerful remarks about how much I reminded them of their moms, or the moms of their friends. I was forty-four. Sometimes at work I was very, very tired.

I'd held on. I believed I did the right thing by waiting for a position to become available that was obviously meant for me. When it arrived, I went for it with everything I had. I loved the new energy pulsing in my body, the new confidence, the currents of a hopefulness I knew was real and true and good.

It can't be true I'm not getting it.

Over and over I kept saying that to myself in a loop I could not bust out of.

The promotion didn't come with an actual office. But it meant a larger cubicle. It meant a window. Since I'd be staying on the same floor, I would still be too low for a view of treetops and sky. But I was going to have a window!

The chair that was supposed to be mine could be positioned so I faced the opening, my eyes seeing straight on, not like in the regular cubicles, where the desk or tabletops were attached to a wall, and the doorways that had no doors were on your side, or behind you.

And then no more of being sneaked up on, right up to me closely.

It wasn't just one guy doing it, while passing through my section from other departments, like they belonged to a club with a hobby. Like this was how anyone would take a little break to have some fun. They weren't the new kids. They were men.

If I wanted to report this, I would not have followed through. I would have felt like a crybaby. I couldn't call it workplace harassment, not when everyone knew what that meant. This wasn't anything *bad*.

Sometimes I let the perpetrator know I wanted him to cut it out, to knock it off, to get away from my space and never return. But I never raised my voice. I didn't want to seem I was about to lose my temper.

I wanted to appear tough-skinned, hard to rattle.

I wanted to look like I was a pro at keeping my cool.

I was one of the guys!

I was fitting in!

There wasn't a pattern. Weeks could go by of nothing. I never heard them approaching. The floor in my department was covered with sound absorbers of spongy tiles.

My concentration would be taken from me. A finger might poke my shoulder. Or there might be a thump to the back of my chair. I jumped up startled every time, as if my breath had been robbed from me too. Then all I could do afterward was feel angry at myself once again for letting myself get spooked.

Hey, Trisha!

BOO!

Eight

When my father was born, he was automatically a Patrick. It was the name of his father, grandfather, and probably ancestors in Ireland way back, burning peat for cooking and heat, and being righteously Gaelic and taking part in rebellions. Also there were uncles and cousins, on my mother's side too, and what was my mother's given name? She was always called Mamie, but officially she was Mary Pat, for a combo of her grandmothers, Maeve Mary and Patricia Bernadette. She had an aunt Patty Lou, and a sister-in-law Patsy, whose daughter was Patsy too.

When I became a person in this world, I became Patricia. My parents would never have considered anything else.

Patricia Eileen Gilley. The Eileen was for my father's godmother. I was branded from the start with family.

When I was small, before the reunions lost their attraction, there were family gatherings held alternately in the Massachusetts places of Dorchester and Revere, and also in southern New Hampshire and coastal Rhode Island. Those gatherings involved picnics at public beaches that were unlawfully commandeered, or an inexpensive rental of a Knights of Columbus hall, because someone belonged to that Knights of Columbus. Such gatherings were very, very large.

And it would be Pat, Patrick, Patty, Pat, Patsy, Paddy all over the place, every time, Paddy Patty Pat like a game for babies.

I was Patty until I wasn't. I'd hear my name called, in what sounded like a cheerful way, like something good was coming. I'd rush to the caller, whoever it was, whatever grown-up, and be disappointed. Who they wanted wasn't me.

"I'm Trisha now. Call me Trisha."

I was seven or eight. I don't remember how I came up with it. But I must have had a good reason. I must have made lists, worked it out: a problem to solve, an answer that was a victory.

One day, when my husband was my boyfriend, he noticed that my initials spelled PEG.

He never told me why he felt so strongly that my parents had named me wrongly, and I should have been Margaret, and nicknamed Peggy or Peg. But trying to explain it to me would mean being rational about it. Which he wasn't.

Did I look like a Peg? Or a Peggy? He thought so.

It happened to come up one day in his car, the two of us just riding around because we both loved riding around. We had a thing for aimless wandering in common, where you don't know what your destination is until you're there. Or there isn't a destination at all and you're just building up momentum for sex. Right from the start, we were really, really good at being compatible with our bodies.

We loved listening to the radio. But we could never agree what station to put it on, so we kept it on scan.

"Peggy Sue" came on one of the oldies stations. He had never revealed warm feelings, or fandom, for Buddy Holly. With a determination that surprised me, he stopped the scan so the song could play. We had a rule that when one of us made a choice, the other one had to go along with it. I was usually the one who went for Buddy Holly, although not that particular song. I detested it for being dumb in how it keeps repeating "pretty, pretty, pretty," which doesn't feel like a way to describe a human. You feel Peggy Sue is the name of, like, a cat.

And out he came with his request. Would it be okay if he started calling me Peg, or Peggy, nickname-like? Based on what he'd just realized my initials were? He wouldn't call me Peggy Sue, though.

His expression was full of sweetness and softness when he turned his head my way at a red light. He said it was just an idea, a spontaneous thing, no big deal. I was free to make fun of him for being ridiculous, if I wanted to.

Which I didn't. We never made fun of each other.

"I'm Trisha," I answered.

Maybe there was something in my voice he hadn't heard before. But he made light of it.

"I get it. You're Trisha! Very cool. Let's go fuck!"

Later, I wondered about it. When we married, I took his name voluntarily, gladly, the same as holding out my hand for him to slip on the gold band, sliding it easily over that knuckle: a perfect fit, a very big deal, *I'm a wife now.*

I would wonder, what if he asked me to change my first name too? It would have been easy when I went officially from Gilley to Donahue, with a new driver's license, new paperwork, a new me. He loved me. I loved him. What if he needed me to become Peg Donahue, or Peggy, like a gift he set his heart on, which only I could give him? Did I want to be a refuser of a gift? Did I want to break his heart?

I would try out the words, for no one's ears but my own.

"I'm Peg."

"I'm Peggy."

Oh, it's only a name and names don't really matter, I'd feel sometimes.

At work now and then, I would ponder the question as I settled into my cubicle at the start of a day, or sat waiting for many pages of a document to finish printing, for whichever high-up in the company refused to read reports online.

Would I? Would I have changed my whole name, if I understood he was asking me to do so because of love?

I didn't know. Asking myself what I would have done was a test I self-administered. I flunked it every time. I just really didn't know.

Nine

One good thing about Banquet Day was that I wasn't at actual work.

I wasn't the only one assuming the promotion was a done deal. Two guys in my department were stuck with each other in sharing a cubicle. On the basis of mine becoming free, they were lobbying for a split-up and a coin toss to see who moved and who stayed. On the afternoon of my first interview—as early as that—I returned to my space to find a message on my desk. It was spelled out in M&M's, the chocolate-mint kind, with shells in various shades of green.

On the counter in my department's little kitchen, there was a serving platter from one of our free lunches, which the caterer had forgotten to take away. So the platter became ours. It held loose M&M's, dark-chocolate mints only. Every day the candy was replenished. No one knew who brought it in, or who filled the platter, in case more than one person was involved. All I knew was that I had nothing to do with it.

The message in candy on my desk said, "CONGRATS BYE DO NOT 4GET US."

I'd only be moving about a hundred feet away. I'd still be connected to the team. Yet the words felt exactly right. I would officially outrank them all, even our manager.

I'd always resisted those candies, as a safeguard against being teased for taking too many, not that I knew what "too many" might mean. But that day, after looking at my message for several happy moments, I devoured the whole thing, and felt a glow.

There was going to be a promotion.

All through the week pre-banquet, no one mentioned what I wasn't getting. The subject was in a blackout. Everyone acted gently polite to me, taking on the manners we adopted when any one of us returned to work from a sickness, family emergency, or funeral.

They knew. My team. They all knew.

Clearly, I'd been shattered. It had to be obvious even to the guys who operated on a basis of "don't bother me with any type of emotional thing whatsoever."

I wasn't being shunned, like, *shunned*. Or isolated as if I carried a disease. It was just all very much a big shock.

And I had a new dilemma. The most efficient path for me to take to the nearest ladies' room meant passing the large cubicle with the window. Which no longer was about to be mine.

The position had been filled. Who it was remained a mystery, at least to me. That cubicle was unoccupied, un-moved-into. But a new computer had arrived. It was right there inside, right there on the desk, in an unopened box.

Walking by, even in a hurry, as I'd long had the habit of waiting too long to get up and go pee, I found it impossible to keep myself from glancing sideways. I would look into the cubicle at the waiting-ness, the stillness, the phantom of myself at that desk, in that chair, wrapped up in a gauze of sunlight. It was like someone in a fairy tale seeing a vision in a crystal ball.

I was the someone and I was the vision too.

Except that, this was not a fairy tale. I was my same old self at work being suddenly afraid of wetting my own pants, because of lingering.

I could not summon the willpower to avert my gaze, to not linger. So I had to stop passing by. I came up with an alternate route. It was longer, which meant I had to recondition myself regarding paying attention to bodily impulses and timing. Which was not a bad thing. I could justify the longer distance by calling it added-on exercise. I could feel I was doing myself a favor by tacking on a few extra indoor minutes to my daily walk outside. I could be satisfied that I'd thought it out, made an adjustment, solved a problem.

Sometimes I accused myself of being small-minded and ridiculous. For counting steps that way, counting minutes that way. Breaking down my life into little unimportant steps and tiny bits of time.

But anything was better than not being able to keep my eyes off that chair, that desk, that new, unopened box, like a gift that had my name on it, but then someone sneaked in and made a swap.

Like I was robbed.

It occurred to me I had the right to be mad. The company had a reputation of promoting from within. After the change in regimes, this was true even more. I was the insider. That job was tailor-made for me, was destined for me. This wasn't only about a broken promise, or a dangling of a reward that was suddenly, with no explanation, yanked away. Or a sort of jilting, like someone being stood up, for some unknown, illogical, stupid, personal reason.

This was about a wrong thing.

I worked on being mad. "Okay, I'm getting mad now," I'd say to myself.

I compared the company to my kids, in the act of some outrageous behavior I needed to put a stop to, with a certain expression, a certain few words, and then a threat to shut down the internet in our household. I was the one who configured it. I knew how to lock it down. I understood the power of putting the internet in a time-out.

It was the only comparison I could think of. But it did me no good. I didn't love the company. I wasn't the company's mom.

After failing to be mad, I went over everything I recalled from the interviews. What words did I say that I shouldn't have said? What wrong expression did my face take on that I was probably unaware of?

What about my clothes, posture, tone of voice? What about the way I walked, the way I sat, the way I turned, the way I stood up?

What about my very self?

And what about my gender?

Ten

When I was a student, I didn't think the amount of a salary would be the single most important thing about finding a job. But that was before the full awareness of my loans kicked in—loans I took out as an undergraduate because the scholarships and financial aid I received, along with part-time jobs, were not enough to pay all those bills. In grad school I was funded during the regular course of semesters, but I needed loans for summer classes and special tutorials, so I could reduce the number of years I was not yet launched into the real world, into my real life.

When the time came, I had to be focused on my own bottom line. How much was the pay? I was offered positions in every company I applied to. The one I chose had seemed so promising.

I went to orientation day apprehensively. It took place in a conference room where I was one of a dozen newbies. There, I was approached by a woman who had just delivered a talk. This woman was only several years older than me, but she was loaded with confidence. She brimmed with it—with that thing that can only be called self-confidence, so hard to get by without, so easy to never have.

This woman gave off strong vibes of worldly experience, and also a company-workplace version of street smarts. And she was perfect. That was the word that came to me, as I felt my own self shrinking: shrinking and being clumsy and nerdy, and truly, profoundly inadequate, maybe not as a new professional, but as a female.

I soon discovered that the woman was a consultant, brought in to introduce us to an early sense of what we were getting into, now that we were entering corporate life. Her talk was based on things like, *How will you put your best foot forward at the start of your career?*

And, *Think of working in a company as your own private process of evolution, just like what Darwin said. You have to maximize your ability to adapt. Think of this as a necessity, if you don't want your career to go extinct.*

She placed special emphasis on the word "adapt." Four other women were in the group, but I was the only one she singled out.

I had believed I looked appropriate in my new navy pantsuit, pin-striped blouse, and basic, square-heeled Oxfords—and what a klutz I was! The woman's suit had a close-fitting, elegant jacket, and a very narrow skirt in a soft pastel of bluish gray. Her blouse was a v-neck, silk, pearly white. It was an outfit you have to dry-clean, not toss in the wash in cold water like mine.

The consultant was a star, I saw, at being feminine.

When she was giving her talk, I had to think about the difference between having a body and having a figure. Between having a haircut and having a hairdo. Between putting on some lipstick and making sure you took care of your facial hair, and wearing makeup on your eyes and your skin that's completely perfect, as if you airbrushed your face like a photo, and maybe your appearance took a long time to achieve, and maybe it didn't.

The woman's legs in her pantyhose looked like they never once grew stubble. Her high heels were especially pointed at the toes, like she was sending a message that putting her best foot forward meant an actual sharp angle.

Like what she wore on her feet could be weaponized.

I was overtaken by an envy I could not rise above. I had the thought that, from now on, for the rest of my life, every time I saw a weed in a beautiful garden, I would have to say, "Hello there, weed. I want you to know I completely understand what it's like to be you."

So this woman, having signaled to me, reached me before I had time to head for an exit. I was sure she planned to offer me advice about my own appearance. Criticism, actually. Which would be, of course, objective, correct, and necessary. I could only hope it would not come too hurtfully.

The woman quietly said, with her face full of warmth, and even admiration, of all things, "Hi. I saw you walk down the hall on your way in. I saw how you were sitting. May I give you a tip?"

Uh-oh, I thought, as if her kind, friendly expression might have been a fake-out.

But she was still smiling at me, even more warmly.

"Sure," I said. "I'll take some advice."

"Did you ever train as a dancer, or a gymnast?"

Oh no, I thought, is she hitting on me?

I had learned from women in the last few years of my life at that time, that if a woman approaches you and extends a suggestion that the two of you should get together, get to know each other sexy-like, and maybe fall in love, the best thing to say is, "Thanks for thinking of me that way! I'm sorry I'm so heterosexual, but wow am I flattered!"

Which I was pretty much prepared to say, and good for me I didn't. I just shook my head, confused. Train as a dancer? Or a gymnast?

I went to a regional high school where girls in sports came from prosperous places, and everyone else put up with just boring, horrible gym classes. I did not dance at all. I had never taken a lesson in anything physical, but in college, I bought a good bike and rode it everywhere, and I swam in the Olympic pool, although never competitively. In grad school I took up jogging, but it was just to work off pressure and stress and being worried all the time about money.

And the woman said, "I asked you those questions because you carry yourself well."

"I do?"

"Trust me. Never change how you walk and how you sit. In other words, keep your head high. Keep your back straight, and your shoulders too. Keep that stride of yours."

No one had ever spoken to me in this manner before. Probably, the company didn't bring her in and pay her a consultant's fee to say these kinds of things.

"And keep looking taller than you are, no matter what's on your feet," the woman added.

"Um, thanks," I managed to say. "Really. It means a lot. Thank you."

"Good luck."

The woman's time at orientation was over. I watched her move toward a door, and I saw what she meant about walking. It was a marvel to me that she pulled off a stride in such heels, in a very tight skirt, with no slits in the fabric. For about four seconds, I had a fantasy of myself as a fashion and style clone of this unexpected, one-time mentor. It felt nice. And then I snapped back to my senses.

After that, I was self-conscious for a while about every movement I made at work. But I came to understand that the woman's advice was the best thing that happened to me in the two years I was part of my first company.

I left that job with a little bit of relief in the weight of my loans, and that was good, and so was owning a car, for the first time in my life. The job had been going along all right, with a steady balance between the ups and the downs. Then one day I went into work and found that I'd been changed from a salaried worker to a pay-by-the-hour one, beginning immediately. I tried to make a go of it, but soon my hours were cut without warning to a level that wasn't officially part-time. And the hours they offered didn't qualify me for health care, or any benefits at all.

I tried to find out if I'd been the only person in my section to be cut. I couldn't just look around and count heads. I wasn't there enough. I asked around and found only a reticence, or an outright lack of engagement, like I was bringing up a subject that was taboo. On my last day there, an administrative assistant who went to my high school, and had always been nice to me, stopped by my desk to say, in a low voice, confidentially, "You know how people that suck at their job can get squashed without outright being fired?"

I sucked at that job? And I had no idea until now?

I said to her, "I suck at my job?"

"Christ, no," she replied. "The opposite."

So I moved on: the girl from the part of the valley where you were expected to stay where you were, to find a job you didn't have to go to college for, as if life had a certain type of pathway, on a certain type of slope. The pathway could be, I'd figured out, a simple walk upward. Or a difficult climb made easier if you started with just the right training. But no matter what, the path and the slope were only supposed to be for other people.

I had wanted to be other people.

"Look taller than you are."

I am a little under five feet six. I have some fleshiness in a thin ruff of skin beneath my chin, but other than that I am lean and angular, and small and still-firm in my breasts, and long in my legs. I have thick brown hair, a little wavy. I've always kept it short. I've worn no makeup to work, ever, except lipstick now and then, if I thought of it. I never had my ears pierced, and I wear no jewelry, not counting my wedding band and a thin gold chain around my neck, with a gold heart, concealed inside my blouses. It opens to tiny photos of my sons, the pair of them, one on each side of the heart.

They both were scrunched-up, downy-headed, astoundingly beautiful newborns.

Those pictures were taken by a hospital photographer for that very purpose. I did not keep pictures of my husband and children on my desk or attached to my cubicle walls. My work space was too packed with work stuff. My husband was the gold on my hand, my kids the gold heart at my chest.

Following my final interview, I went back to my cubicle and tapped my wedding ring against the side of my computer, like I was sending my husband a message of good news, in secret code. Then I pulled out my locket. I popped it open and whispered to my kids, like the photos were alive, "Guys, I did it! Hello, promotion. I totally nailed this thing."

Eleven

My husband's parents didn't like me. Neither did his two sisters and their husbands.

We didn't see any of them regularly. That wasn't my fault. The version of my husband that appeared in their presence had little to do with who he was. Sitting at a table with all of them for some holiday or birthday, I could almost feel I was cheating on him with another man, even though the other man was him, and someone I couldn't stand.

It was as if my husband had a real-life avatar that resembled him like an identical twin. Stepping into this alternate persona meant going back to being the guy he used to be, in the entire part of his life before he met me.

He'd go stiff in his backbone, spare in the words he spoke, and sort of vacant in his eyes, like he was gazing beyond all those people he was related to, and looking instead at some distant view only visible to himself. And he would become polite—extremely, insufferably *polite*.

He'd wonder later why our kids, before they were old enough to figure out what was going on, misbehaved at those gatherings with a zeal and a gleeful intensity they never worked up anywhere else.

To his credit, when they did something awful at a Donahue table, like make farting noises in a moment of quiet, or refuse to eat anything on their plates they didn't like, which would sometimes be the whole meal, he allowed them to notice a certain look on his face that told them he was proud of them. They loved being banished to the kitchen, although his family truly thought it was a punishment.

I was all right with the politeness, with all of it. I stuck close to the stranger he turned into. I had to believe he'd work things out with himself eventually. It was only a few times a year, and only based on his sense of duty as a son and a brother, and anyway, the avatar died a ritualistic death on the car ride home. He'd whisper to me that all was well. In his head, he'd killed it. Again. I only asked once about the method. Low-tech, very medieval, with a sword, very King Arthur, he told me. I had to stop him from going into graphic descriptions of how it all went down.

Sometimes, before the position at work opened up for my promotion, I felt I might have made a mistake in setting up the rule that we would take no further handouts from his parents.

Like we were their charity. But how could two people hold good jobs and bring in good salaries, and then money would run through their fingers like they'd plunged their hands into a fast-moving river?

But we were so lucky to have college accounts for our kids. And two nice cars we always traded in before they looked used. And dinner out whenever we wanted, and we didn't bother caring what the prices were. And it was normal to order, instead of glasses, a whole bottle of wine, at a crazy-unbelievable price, which used to shock me.

Never once did my husband begrudge the money we sent every month to my mother and father in their retirement complex. The more they aged, the more they were going to need from us. He would never even think of not being there for them financially.

He loved it that, when I brought him to meet them, the first thing they asked was, "Are you a Democrat?"

I'd already described his parents and sisters to them, including their political affiliation. They were prepared to believe he could not be trusted. They weren't satisfied with his very emphatic, "Yes, of course I am."

My parents and I weren't close. Or we were close in my early years, and it evaporated. But we had "Democrat" in common.

In the restaurant we took them to, which they'd never been in before, or anywhere like it, they quietly bombarded him with questions they'd carefully prepared earlier, without my knowledge. Like they believed I'd bring a Republican into their lives, never mind mine.

I'd forgotten to warn him that they were political. But I remembered to tell him not to bring up the subject of a certain family, and especially the presidency of a member of that family, John Fitzgerald Kennedy, whose name they always uttered in full, with the reverence they would have given to a saint, if they both hadn't washed their hands of religion a long time ago. They weren't just Democrats. They were Massachusetts Democrats. They were just the right age that, if you mentioned a Kennedy, there would go the evening.

It was more than enough that they quizzed him. How did he feel about this? How did he feel about that? Was he giving honest answers, or was he messing around with the truth, in order to make a good impression?

They were a little intimidated by him, but they were also acting like bigots, and they were proud of themselves for doing so, just because he wore clothes they felt were unbelievably expensive. They didn't know he wasn't wearing any of his really costly things, on purpose. They had to establish his whole voting record as far back as he could remember, before they ordered their steaks.

At his own workplace, my husband was already as high up as he wanted to go. He received regular increases in pay. He had no complaints about his compensation. He didn't love his work, but he didn't dislike it on a chronic, everyday basis. He was *settled*.

Only once did he mention looking forward to my promotion in terms of money.

It was almost a casual statement, spoken lightly one evening when he felt like stacking the dishwasher after dinner instead of leaving it to me, which was fine, as he was a much better stacker. He took that sort of thing seriously.

He felt I should know that he'd been thinking about cutting back his hours. It was no big deal. He'd still be employed in his job full-time. Or, actually, full-time that was a few hours short of normal, regular full-time.

He wanted to be at home more. Not to work at home, but be home, like, *home*. To fix things, to do stuff around the house. He didn't know how to fix anything. He had never learned basic home maintenance. He could barely change a light bulb!

He wanted our kids to know house stuff too! If his paycheck got reduced, so what!

We'd have my promotion to make up for it! Everything would balance out!

Twelve

In spite of my efforts, I failed to figure out in hindsight any deal-breaker mistakes of mine in my interviews for the promotion.

I would have dressed special for them, if I had the chance. Each of the meetings took place when I was at work already. I didn't know the day ahead of time. The only prior notice I was given took the form of a phone call or email from HR, with information about the hour and location. I thought about choosing outfits and fixing myself up to look interview-ready every day, just in case.

But I knew what kind of teasing I'd be in for, if I showed up every morning looking spiffy and kind of formal. Or even if I went a few days not wearing jeans. Maybe there are lots of people in workplaces and other group situations who know how to deal with suddenly being made fun of, for some reason that's never a reason really.

I never had the good luck of growing the second skin you need to withstand being openly mocked. Which you're supposed to laugh about! Like, that was only someone playing a joke, and wow, it was really funny!

Once, about a year before I didn't get the promotion, a high-up in the company was contacted by the agency that ran the online classes I took now and then.

These classes were difficult. There was no penalty for dropping out before completion—in fact, you'd get an email praising you for however far you got, with an invitation to join again sometime. I had to pay for the classes in full, up front, myself. My company refused to pay the bill. Yes, sure, it was good for them that I was always learning new things. But the classes were voluntary, not assigned. The agency was good about reimbursement of the remaining tuition when someone had to hit the button saying they'd had enough and could not go on, thanks, goodbye.

I never didn't finish a class.

A representative of the agency had wanted the high-up in my company to know that of everyone who completed the class I had just completed, I was in a small group of top performers. They'd broken it down into fourths. I'd finished in the top quarter. A lot of people in the world, I knew, had taken that particular class.

Well, not a lot, like, not huge numbers in general. Just a lot of professionals doing what I did, or something similar.

I was in the top one-fourth *globally*.

In the breakdown of countries, in the figures pertaining to the United States, they gave percentages. I was in the top ten percent.

The agency's message to my company was a note of congratulations. I did not receive such a thing myself.

The high-up forwarded the congratulations and the praise to the office that handles public relations and newsletters. The information was included in a regular electronic bulletin within the company. I didn't know it would appear. I rarely even glanced at those things.

In my department there was little reaction at first. Just a mention from my manager that I ought to take a look at the latest issue. He raised a fist to pump the air.

He said to me, "Way to go!"

Shortly afterward, previous to a regular department meeting, someone wrote something on the big whiteboard. It was customarily blank when we entered that conference room.

I happened to be the last to arrive. There'd been a delay for me. I was asked by a member of my team to hold off leaving my cubicle, so I could look over a memo he wanted another pair of eyes on. He left me alone with it. Later it occurred to me that he'd set me up.

On the whiteboard, one sentence had been written over and over, in printed letters, all capitals. The style and form immediately conjured only one correct reference. It was pretty direct. Unless you'd never seen *The Simpsons,* you could not look at that board without seeing how the writer of the words had copied Bart with a piece of chalk in his hand, in his classroom, carrying out a punishment on the blackboard for things he was supposed to stop doing, like giving wedgies, pretending to have rabies, telling his fellow pupils their teacher was not wearing underpants.

Twenty-two times. The sentence about me had been written twenty-two times. I counted.

"WE MUST NOT CALL TRISHA MISS SMARTY PANTS."

There was laughter and applause as I read the board, as I counted.

Hey, Lisa Simpson!

Don't get a swelled head!

Trisha! How much would you charge for the cheat notes you used?

Aw, do we have to erase it?

I didn't laugh. I acted like I was ignoring them, along with what was written.

There came to me the secret feeling that I was a coward. I was saying to myself, "Do not go to that board and tip it over and tell everyone in this room they are horrible people, and they deserve hell, which is hopefully a real place, just so they can go there."

And I was saying, "Do not, do not, do *not* start to cry."

And I was saying, "Be brave!"

While knowing it did me no good, like I didn't understand what the word even meant.

Thirteen

The first of my three promotion interviews took place in HR, a department with almost a whole floor of its own, and spacious hallways and offices and cheerful side-rooms, not cubicles. It seemed that the first priority of Human Resources was to let everyone know they deserved the right to plush accommodations.

In a cozy little room, very homey, with lamps and a sofa and armchairs, I was met by a senior manager who wanted to make sure my file was current and accurate. Then I was informed what the new salary and benefits would be.

Like I already had the job.

I thought so because that was the way I was spoken to.

I found out from the manager that no one else was being considered for the position. That was a courtesy to me, based on my standing in the company and my number of years with them. My eight years made me senior in terms of length of employment, especially since many employees left their jobs, voluntarily or not, when the new regime began. I also had the feeling from this manager, a woman, that the promotion probably should have been given to me quite some time earlier.

When she left the happy little living room, she was replaced by the man who would become my new boss.

With him, it wasn't a question and answer sort of thing, but a conversation. It seemed to me he had many other things on his mind while talking to me, and now and then he'd lose track of what he was saying. But I felt our conversation was a good one. I'd heard that as a boss, he was decent and fair. He had a reputation for trusting people he supervised to know what they were doing, with little input from him. And he let me know that his boss-ness of me would really be *pro forma*. I'd still be connected to my team. Overseeing the new position had been slotted into his turf, and that was fine, but he already had a lot on his plate.

I walked away with confidence. That was the day I went back to my section and the candies were on my desk, and I ate the message.

Which did not cancel out the whiteboard incident. But I was not going to allow bitterness to take root inside me. I was not going to be resentful. I was going to keep on moving on.

The second interview was with the man who was that man's boss. I was notified as soon as I arrived on that day that I should go to his office at four. I felt grateful for the extra notice. For the first interview, I only had about an hour to prepare.

So, okay, all good, four in the afternoon.

But at a little after ten thirty, the boss of my expected new boss showed up in my department's kitchen. He had tracked me there.

I was standing by the counter, trying to decide if I should put the kettle on for tea, or save time by sticking a mug of cold water in the microwave. Besides that, should I go with an herbal? Should I never mind herbal and choose an extra jolt of caffeine? My regular latte, at ten past nine, was far from wearing off. I knew I would need to caffeine up again later on, closer to the interview time. I was always so draggy at four o'clock.

Maybe I made an impression on that boss as someone too daydreamy to be promoted.

He had startled me, appearing so suddenly, so unusually. High-ups did not in the normal course of things go sniffing out employees in their own areas. I could not think of any other time someone entered the kitchen who was not a member of my department.

He wanted to know, right away, what was up with the plate of candy on the counter? Were they breath mints?

From where he stood, he couldn't see the markings of M&M. I told him what brand they were.

He didn't seem to believe me. But why would I lie about a small round piece of chocolate encased in a candy shell, when he could have picked one up to examine it?

"They can't be," he pointed out. "They're all green."

"It's the chocolate mints kind," I said.

"Where did they come from?"

"They sort of just appear."

"What do you mean?"

"It's a mystery. No one's ever been caught."

"I see," said the boss of my almost new boss. "That platter, is it one of the caterer's?"

"It is. They forgot it after one of our lunches."

Maybe he thought someone in my department had stolen it. Maybe he thought the culprit was me.

Next, to my surprise, he announced that he'd attended a meeting in another section on my floor. He had decided to walk me to his office, seeing as he was headed that way.

For the interview.

It took me a moment to understand the interview was with me, and it was about to happen. I was proud of myself for becoming instantly alert, for rising to the occasion. I was glad to be wearing my nicest black pants, new enough that the pleats below the waist were still pleats without having to be ironed, which I avoided to the point of ironing never. The blouse I wore was one of my best. It was too early in the day for me to have gone outside for a walk, so I didn't have to worry if I was fresh.

His office was only one floor up. He was a devoted stair-walker, he informed me. But would I prefer the elevator?

"Oh, no. I don't need to ride," I answered.

Did he think I was lazy? An avoider of physical movement? Obviously he had never seen me getting in my exercise along the office park pathways. Or he had seen me but took no notice of me, since I was only some random employee, out in the air.

I had never interacted directly with this man before. It did not feel strange to me that he didn't speak to me on the way.

A long hallway had to be traveled before reaching our destination. When we came to the top of the one flight of stairs, he was ahead of me, and held the door open. I thanked him. I stepped into the hall a few paces, pausing for him to catch up.

When he did, he kept going, breezing by me.

Now came my turn to play catch-up. He was fit and vigorous, somewhere in his fifties. He had an inch or two on me in height. He had a long, powerful stride. About halfway there, he glanced sideways, and seemed startled that I was beside him, keeping up. By the look on his face, he seemed to feel I'd done something wrong, that I had broken a rule.

The interview was fairly short. It turned out to be all right, in a mellow sort of way. Would I describe my recent projects? My history with the company? How I'd handle the new position?

I was convinced the company was simply going through the right motions, following protocol, keeping it professional, in spite of making me feel a little weirded out by the unprofessional business with scheduling me.

He didn't rise from his chair at the end of our meeting to shake hands with me. That was due to one of his administrative assistants coming into his office to inform him he needed to join an important video conference, that very moment. That was how I knew the interview was over. I didn't feel slighted, although I should have. I walked away with the sense of a done deal, just as I felt eight years ago on the day I accepted the company's offer to employ me. Like I'd been recruited for a second time.

Yes!

The third, final interview was the shortest, with a very high-up executive who interrupted me several times to take phone calls. He told me that talking with him was a mere formality—he'd heard excellent things about me. It was a bonus to his day he had the chance to meet me!

Two days later, I returned to my cubicle from a routine meeting to find a message from HR, sent just minutes earlier. It was an email from their general address. There was no signature line, no name.

Please would I come to that department, at my convenience?

Which to me was right away. But I made myself sit tight for a while. I didn't want to seem too eager about accepting my new position.

As soon as I arrived on that floor, I found it difficult to make sense of what was going on, like walking into a theater and a film is playing in a language you don't know. And there are no subtitles. And you don't even know what country it's in.

I was steered to the office of a man who was new. He looked to be in his early twenties. I might have been the first employee he delivered a decision to.

He was a smooth talker, wanting me to believe that, at heart, he was a really nice guy. He was casual in his manner, and eager to make it seem he understood the basic fact that there were sides in the company—two sides, them and us. He wanted me to think he was an "us." That the side he was on was mine.

He called me Mrs. Donahue. He complimented me for being a totally terrific asset to the company, a totally solid employee.

And then it was something like, Mrs. Donahue, here's the thing! You're so great in your current position, the company needs to keep you there! It's been decided high up that the job you have now can't possibly be done half as well by anyone else! You are so, so valued!

That was the whole of it. Once again I went back to my cubicle. I gathered my handbag, briefcase, and jacket. I left the building without a word to anyone.

It was midafternoon. I didn't want to show up at home early and have to explain myself. I drove to a park with a pond, two suburbs away from mine. My husband and I used to take the kids here when they were tiny. There used to be ducks.

The kids were enchanted by the ducks. They'd seen pictures of mallards in their storybooks, out of water as well as in, so they knew you couldn't be a waterfowl and not have skinny little legs and webbed feet.

But these ducks were special. There were no legs and feet beneath the surface. There was no wind to propel them. These ducks were happily gliding around because they had magical powers no other ducks possessed.

Who knew how or why they'd come up with that, but who cared? My husband and I developed the habit of never letting them witness a duck coming out onto land, which was tricky, because people were always offering human food to the gliders. We'd turn their heads or just leave. We wanted the magic, too.

This day was cool, bright, breezy. I could not believe there was sunlight. I could not believe the whole world wasn't covered in shadows.

I sat in my car and wondered what happened to the ducks, even though I realized I would never be able to find out. I watched people walking around, doing normal things: pushing a stroller, throwing a stick for a dog, conversing in a friendly way on a bench.

I started to cry the moment after I parked there. They were hot, stinging tears, lots and lots of them. I had to turn on the radio to cover the sounds I was making. Then I had to turn on the heater and point the vents straight at me, to dry the top front of my clothes. But by the time I walked into my house, my eyes held no telltale wetness, or redness.

Mom's home!

My husband had made chili, and it was, as usual, unspicy. I didn't like hot, biting seasoning in my food. To the surprise of my family, for the first time ever, I asked for the jar of hot sauce to be passed to me, so I could pour some into my bowl.

The burning sensations in my mouth and throat were worth it, as an explanation for why my eyes were watering. I'd been worried I might burst into tears at the table. I didn't have the energy to invent some excuse why. It was not a possibility to tell the truth.

I said yes when my husband offered to open a beer for me, which normally I wouldn't do. I didn't like what it always did to my gut. But he felt a little beer would be perfect for a novice at fiery food like me, now that I was brave enough to eat some heat.

After a few sips of the beer, I was burping my head off. Some surplus foam or the beer itself started coming out of my nose, and it was, oh my God, that looks like snot, Mom! Hey, Mom! Hey, Babe! We love you! It's like a party in here tonight!

Fourteen

On past Banquet Days, with my department, I rode to the Rose & Emerald on the leading shuttle in the convoy. Arriving first made it easier to secure our seating preference of a table with no one but us.

This day, when I made it to the office park barely in time to catch not the first bus but the last, I was the last employee to board. The lead bus had already departed the parking lot. So everyone in my department assumed I was home in the role of a truant, and of course they would think so, given my situation.

Like they'd feel I did not have the guts to be tough.

Like I was churning inside myself with bitter resentment like spoiled milk.

Like I was crying, alone, probably in my bed, as I must have retreated there, must have been all curled up with myself and my pillow and maybe a couple of sedatives. And I'd allow the company to hit me with a future punishment for playing hooky.

Which no way was going to happen.

Up I went, confidently, I thought, up the few steps of the last bus. If I had only looked straight ahead when I entered the aisle, I would not have seen him sitting there, right in front. I had no reason to put the blame on him, but in that moment, I did.

He was in an aisle seat. Next to him, at the window, sat another executive, a high-up who was higher than him, around the rank of general or admiral if this were the military. The two of them were facing each other and quietly talking.

The man in the aisle seat was the boss of the man who was going to be my new boss, and now would never be. He had no idea I was right beside him.

What if, when he showed up in my department's kitchen to tell me that his interview with me was about to happen, more than half a day earlier than scheduled, I looked him in the eyes and refused to go along with the change? What if I said I wanted to stick to the appointed time? I could have come up with the right words to make it seem I was gently offering a reminder of the meeting plan set up by his own office. Maybe I could have phrased this as nothing close to implying I was telling him he'd made an error.

And why should that even be a thing, this whole cumbersome, ridiculous thing of *be careful to never let a man get mad at you for stepping out of line*?

But the truth was, in that situation, if I wanted to stick up for myself, I would not have been able to think quickly. Not able to make a response I could be proud of later. All I could do at the time was see that it would be a good idea to let him know I could follow a command.

In other words, obey him.

Standing in the aisle, so close to him, I paused to catch my breath. I had rushed to make it to the convoy. I'd been nervous about driving to the office park while wearing high heels I'd never worn before, but I couldn't dare leave home in sneakers and take extra time to switch what was on my feet.

I needed to walk to the back of the bus to get a seat. In the pause, I was gearing up for that.

The man of my second interview was pointing out the window in the direction of the new hotel's construction site. A crane was there, high in the sky, darkly metallic, its iron mouth open like a toothy, mega-giant reptile you might see in a movie, and maybe you'd find yourself in a mood to take its side, and cheer for it to be victorious against any humans who needed to be, say, stomped on.

Another load of dirt had just been moved to the hill that was being created for the hotel. That was what these two were watching. I couldn't make out the words of their conversation, until I realized they were talking about the Rose & Emerald.

The Rose & goddamn Emerald, it was. Like goddamn Thanksgiving again this year with someone's crazy goddamn grandmother out in the goddamn country, and shit on a plate for food. And goddamn it, this would be the last time, and thank God for the new hotel for next year, where they'd have a chef who went to a goddamn five-star cooking school and the food would be *gourmet.*

In his seat, with his head turned away from me, he was relaxed and slightly angled. He had stretched out his legs into the aisle. He did not seem aware that no one could get by without stepping over him. Or he might have been aware of that, and could not have cared less.

I was inches from him. The driver had started the engine. The door had whooshed shut. Lifting a foot to cross over the obstacle I'd met up with, I felt myself coming to a boil, as if my blood had been actually heated, the same as water in a kettle on a stove.

I almost spoke to those men. I thought I should defend the Rose & Emerald. But if I opened my mouth to speak, I would sound like my department's kettle when it went off. The whistle was unusually loud and shrill. We had a rule that if you boiled water for tea or cocoa or instant noodles or whatever, you had to take it off the burner before the whistle started screaming. You had to stand in the kitchen by the kettle and pay attention to it.

Staying quiet, with my foot in the air, with the spike of my high heel, I wanted to act. I felt a rush of energy and desire. I wanted to lift my foot higher for more power, then bring it down to the shin of the blocker of my way.

My hands became fisted. My nails as usual were not long or sharp, but they were pressing into my skin. I contained myself. The bus was ready to roll. The moment in which I could have attacked him had passed.

I stepped over him casually, no big deal. And I did a conversion. The boiling of my blood became adrenaline, for making it fast to the rear without falling over. I sank into a seat where I didn't have to sit next to anyone. I congratulated myself. What was going on inside me had stayed inside. I accepted that as a victory.

But I had to wonder, would my spike have drawn blood from his leg?

How deep would it have to go for blood to appear?

Would I have seen it was necessary to place my foot so that the spike of my shoe came in contact with bare skin, not fabric? In fact, some of his skin had been exposed, between a pant cuff and a sock. It was just a tiny patch, but it might have made a good target.

Would the blood trickle down toward his ankle in a small, weak stream, thin as a string? Or would it become a gusher, brightly red and very dramatic, very alarming, very life-threatening?

Fifteen

As I stepped up to the narrow porch at the entrance to the banquet hall, the one the Rose & Emerald called a New England veranda, I remembered the company's rule about shutting off your phone.

My phone was in my handbag. But I couldn't check the settings. I did not have my phone. I did not have my bag.

The lightweight cardigan I'd grabbed in my hurry earlier had an inside pocket with a zipper. In there was the metal ring with my house and car keys. I was wearing the sweater even though the weather was a little too warm for it. The fabric was a cotton blend, but it looked woolly and thick.

I had left my things in my car, in the parking lot at the office park.

My car had self-locked. The parking lot had security cameras everywhere. I didn't need to worry about a theft.

And I remembered I'd shut off my phone before leaving home. I'd received several voice mails and texts from members of my team, and one from my manager too, about the banquet this very day. I was going to attend, right? I would have informed someone if I wasn't going to be there, right?

I answered none of them. Also, it had crossed my mind I would need to prevent my husband from getting hold of me. Usually he and I talked in my car when I was on my way to work, and he'd been wrapped up in his day for several hours. I did not have the ability at this time to carry on a conversation with him. Like everything was normal.

But I'd had the presence of mind to text him from my car before driving away.

I was honest about the wording. It was Banquet Day. Sorry I hadn't told him. I should be home at my regular time. Don't call. Phones have to be off in the hall. Love!

During my commute in, we used the opportunity in a practical way to talk about our children, and not about their excellent general health and strength and well-being—never that, never, "Look how lucky they are!" It was always about whichever child was having trouble or special issues. There was always some odd new mood, or one or both of them were getting over some temporary sickness or an injury, or a screwup at school, or slacking off in terms of grades, which my husband felt I ought to be careful discussing, since I was the one who believed that the whole point of going to school was studying and learning and doing the effort and getting the best grades you could.

It wasn't okay to nag about grades!

But I was willing to argue that it was okay from my own point of view, on the basis of being half the partnership in this parenting thing.

Not to mention how mine was the body with the eggs that were actually *required*. In order for our babies *to be made*. Mine was the body they came out of! I was literally their ancestral home! All my husband did was come up with some sperm!

I would have to tell him again and again I was not a nag.

Our children were not in special education, did not have learning disabilities of any kind, did not come from homes where frictions and daily family awfulness kept other kids from, like, memorizing the names of capitals in American states.

And not even all of them at once.

First, they were required to stick to states beginning with the letters A to M. The teacher broke it down for a test they had a ton of time to prepare for: just those cities in just those states.

All the capitals at once on a test, my children felt, was too much to ask for. It had to be Alabama to Montana only.

Then Nebraska to Wyoming later on, which didn't even divide the list in two exactly, fifty states, twenty-five and twenty-five. Because m has so many states.

So the list isn't equal! So children in that school were being taught it doesn't matter if there is equality! Just because it was subtle and indirect didn't mean it wasn't happening!

"They value equality," my husband told me. "How can they not value that kind of thing, being kids of *us*?"

And home would come a son with a test score of capitals so low, any parent would be saying, "This is not okay."

And the older brother of that son did the same thing two years earlier.

And my husband would say, "You guys keep reminding me of me! Don't be like me! Be like Mom!"

He almost didn't know this was Banquet Day. He didn't know I'd stayed home and I was playing truant but then I wasn't. He didn't know this major thing about me. The same was true for my children. To them, this was a normal morning, Mom at her job, same as ever, a good routine in place, everything secure, everything going just fine.

Like this was any day I had not been informed about the promotion.

My husband had asked about it, four days after the new man-boy in HR delivered the blow he'd delivered to me, and then I went to the pond that had no ducks anymore, and I could never know what happened to the ducks.

"Babe, aren't they taking too long to tell you they're finally upgrading you?"

I'd let him know that my promotion was a subject I needed to avoid. I didn't feel like a liar. I had never concealed anything from him before. I would have thought I'd be terrible at it, not brilliant.

And now I was entering the banquet.

I was not the last one inside. A few stragglers who had lingered to take photos of the views were behind me. I reached into the bowl of numbers in the vestibule like nothing was on my mind except following the rules in a well-behaved manner.

The table for my number was near the center of the banquet hall. I saw that I didn't know anyone already seated there. I did a good job of pretending that I didn't know, from one quick glance inside, the members of my department, including our manager, were together at a table up front. They were on the side of the room opposite the wall of draped windows that could have shown spires of the evergreens in the forest, and the mountain in the distance, like a dream of a hill you longed to travel to, and all the white clouds puffing slowly by, in a blue, very blue, peaceful sky.

Not today. The window drapes were closed. That wall was covered by heavy green velvet material, scruffy here and there from wear and tear, but not so worn out to show any traces of sunlight.

I didn't see my own team, I pretended.

I was getting the hang of walking expertly in those shoes. I made my way to my seat uneventfully. I sat down and nodded a general hello, noting that these strangers did not include anyone I'd been a passenger with on the bus.

Even better, no one among my new table companions worked in HR. Or was a boss or high-up I had interviewed with. I was a clean slate to these people.

Maybe I'd been affected, or spooked, by what happened on the bus with my high heels and the shin of that man in the aisle—or, what *didn't* happen. It occurred to me it might be a good idea to slip out of my shoes.

The tables in the hall were round. Some were for ten place settings, some for eight or six. They were randomly placed. I was at a six, but like all the non-tens, the tablecloth was too big. All the tablecloths were sized for the biggest tables. So a lot of fabric was in overlaps. This table was also kind of low. The cloth descended almost to the floor, stopping just a couple of inches short. Which meant I could get my feet out of those shoes. No one would know. Freed, my feet would not be visible.

I thought for a moment I might have to reach down and pry off the shoes. I only realized now how tight they were. But I had a tiny triumph in being able to work each one off with the other foot.

And I began to look forward, in a familiar, emotional way, to what I might order.

I hadn't eaten anything yet. At home, when I still wasn't going to the banquet, and I was completely in a zone of my own about why I would need to play truant, I sat for breakfast with my kids as usual. But I only had coffee. In my state of mind at that time, for the first time ever, perhaps, I didn't require them to read out loud to me the ingredients on the packs of sausage Hot Pockets they grabbed from the freezer and heated up in the microwave, along with something called French Toast Sticks, which they doused with overly sugary, fake syrup, when right there on the counter was a tin of the real stuff, brought home by me from a farmers' market. Which they scorned.

Sometimes in the afternoons, my husband did the grocery shopping with the kids. Or he phoned for a delivery and let them prepare the lists.

On these lists, in this shopping, in these deliveries, items came into our home I never would have allowed. The one thing I could do was insist they all knew what they were putting into their bodies, in terms of ingredients that had nothing to do with real food. They must have been pleased that I just sat there and watched them fill up on the Hot Pockets and the Sticks.

Sometimes breakfast could get a little touchy. I didn't want to fight with my kids that morning. I didn't want to fight with anyone at all.

Sixteen

Bye, Mom!

See you, Mom!

Love you!

Love you too!

Love you!

Love you too!

Any normal morning, it was, in its motions, last-minute scrambles, backpacks full of stuff, a mini-fight over a T-shirt that had to be changed because I spotted a stain that hadn't come out in the wash. Then a rush to the door for the school van that cost extra, when I had thought it was included in their tuition.

I had planned to fix myself a proper brunch, just for one. Alone in the house, I felt that the day was opening around me full of promise, full of quiet.

The hours ahead seemed a gift. I was holding time in my hands like a gift wrapped up with a bow. I had given the gift to myself, and I was about to open it.

Ten minutes after the school van disappeared to the outside world, I jumped off the living room sofa where I had settled in to *lounge*. I had realized I would not be able to deal with knowing my name was on the list of employees copping out of the banquet.

And up I had stepped to the last bus, out of breath, pausing.

In a magazine I happened upon online, around the time I was nearing forty, I found an article about middle age and emotions. It was written by a psychologist who made the case that, when you reach the end of your thirties and leave your youth behind, there is no such thing as experiencing emotions you haven't already had.

The article was bleak. But I was impressed with how convincing it seemed. Once you enter the dimension of being post-young, you can only experience variations of feelings that happened before.

Imagine emotions, the psychologist suggested, as letters of the alphabet. At A, you're brand new. At Z, you're thirty-nine. After that, for the rest of your life, the letters can form words that were not already in your vocabulary. But you don't get any more letters.

That, I now knew, was wrong.

One day, at the age of fifteen, at a lake where I went swimming with my girl gang, I became separated from them after staying in the water when we heard the ice-cream truck arriving in the parking lot. My friends went rushing off to meet it.

I was fine with being suddenly on my own. I'd been trying to work up the courage to venture out to the raft, quite far from shore—you had to be a proper swimmer, I had felt, in order to make it.

I'd been studying swim strokes, without telling anyone. I badly wanted to go to the raft. I wanted to dive off it into deep water, like the kids who showed up sometimes and you could tell they'd had proper swimming lessons, with a proper instructor, starting from when they were tiny. My friends called them stuck-up, asshole preppies. Who took it for granted they were better than all the rest of us.

Secretly, I admired them in the water, so smooth with their movements, so agile, so Olympic-like.

The ice-cream truck's loudspeaker was blasting one of its little-kid songs. I could seize the moment. I would swim to the raft right then and there.

I decided to alternate a front crawl and backstroke, for starters. No one was out on the raft. The preppies were gathered together around picnic tables at the other side of the sandy-beach area where we hung out.

I made it to the raft. It was wood boards polished smooth from water, on a floating platform of barrels. I pulled myself up and dropped to the wood in exhaustion, for a rest. I loved the feel beneath me of the bobbing raft. I loved the little, muted splashes of the lake. I loved how proud of myself I suddenly was.

I didn't know the man who so suddenly appeared beside me—then behind me, when I sat up. He was right up close to my back. His body blocked mine. I knew I could not be seen from the shore. No one was swimming in the shallows of the lake. I was alone with this man.

He was old enough to be someone's father, possibly even old enough to be the father of a grown-up. He could have been someone's grandfather. His face was prickly-stubbly with a short, short beard. I would never see him again.

He was whispering something to me.

He was whisper-crooning words about how glad he was that I had picked up his signals about meeting him here. I had no idea what he was talking about. I hadn't noticed him on the shore, or anywhere else. Was he a pervert, a letch, a creep? He didn't seem so. He looked as normal as any normal man. His hand grabbed my right breast, squeezing me. I squirmed to get away, and found that he was holding me in a lock. I knew, as his hand moved downward, I would never wear a two-piece suit again. I never did.

He was fit and strong: a very tan white man, a powerful and experienced swimmer, obviously. I was able to take action as he shifted a bit to raise me up a little, the better to get his fingers inside my suit, where no one's hands had ever gone except my own.

I bit him. Hard.

I knew as it happened I would never forget what it was like when my teeth dug into the flesh of his inside upper arm.

I did not feel a desire to cause him pain.

There was no "I want to."

It was purely kinetic. I was a kid, going on instinct, going on a wild courage, a wild necessity, like an animal, purely reacting.

Afterward, I didn't wonder if I gave him a wound that might cause him to bleed.

The shock of the bite unloosened his grip. I had just enough time to dive and get away. It didn't matter I had never jumped in an arc, headfirst, into the deep part of the lake. It was a good dive. By the time I was making my way to the shore, my friends were wading into the water and splashing around, seeing me, calling to me.

I looked back once toward the raft. The man was still there, sitting at the far edge, facing the woods on the opposite side. He was still there when we packed up our stuff to go home.

I never told anyone except my husband what had happened. He looked at me, when I did, with a look I'd never seen before. He and I weren't even engaged yet, but I already knew something about love, something so new, I was quietly amazed I'd made it so far in my life without ever feeling anything remotely like it. He told me that if he'd been one of those preppies at the picnic tables, he would have noticed me swimming outward.

He would have admired my strokes. He would have wanted to join me.

And if he'd been there and hadn't seen me swimming, probably because preppie kids in that section were always getting high or drinking sodas with rum or something poured into the cans, he might have broken away from his friends for a trip to the raft himself. And maybe he would have arrived in time to witness me in the act of fighting my attacker. He would have hoped that I bit the man so well, so deeply, blood was drawn, and a scar might have formed, which might have lasted forever.

"They brought me an ice cream, my girlfriends," I told my not-yet-husband, as the last thing to say about that day.

I will always remember the moment I was handed a melting, drippy cone. When I took a lick, the taste of that man's skin was in my mouth no longer.

And so that was my one experience to draw on, to check as a point of reference. A data point.

I needed to figure out if the way I felt that day, at fifteen, precisely in the moment of the bite, fit into the psychologist's theory. I had to know if my response to the man on the raft formed a letter of my own emotional alphabet, which would later spawn a variation. Which would prove that the article was correct.

Working out this problem took up time on the ride from the office park to the Rose & Emerald.

Of the two episodes I was comparing, I had to acknowledge the common element of luck. First, I was lucky on the raft to break free before my assaulter could deliver payback to me, for the bite. And there, I had water to escape to. I also had witnesses—my girl gang—to help me if that man had tried to come after me.

Second, on the bus, with the spike of my shoe, I was lucky I had managed to restrain myself.

Maybe, I concluded, it isn't stupid to imagine an alphabet of feelings.

But no way could such a thing be finite.

The psychologist was a quack. The article was junk data. There can always be new emotions, which don't need to be given labels, signifiers. You can just acknowledge them, absorb them. I had worked it out. When I lifted my foot and wanted to impale the leg of the high-up, I definitely, *most very definitely,* experienced something I'd never experienced before.

I had wanted to hurt him.

Seventeen

I could skip the onion rings. I was attracted to the idea of the macaroni and cheese, as it was mac and cheese for grown-ups, not the stuff from boxes and cans my husband made for our meals.

I could maybe have it as a side dish, although it would mean less room for dessert. I might want to go for something at the dessert buffet I could top with whipped cream, which wasn't the artificial foam my kids begged for, so they could squirt it from the aerosol can into their mouths, then all over each other's clothes and into each other's hair. And up each other's noses if such a thing could be managed. Whenever my husband was in charge of grocery buying, he bought that stuff.

I'd be, "Fine! Have your fun! But I'm killing the internet in here! I'm vaporizing wi-fi for a week!"

The Rose & Emerald whipped its own cream. In the past, I felt I needed to ration how much I took. I didn't want to be made fun of for overdoing it. I'd been afraid to look like an overeating, sweets-addicted person who was putting on tons of weight right in front of everyone's eyes.

But holding self-restraint with the desserts?

Not today.

I could take as many trips as I wanted to the buffet.

I could stuff myself like someone at a bar ordering drink after drink and getting drunk, but it wouldn't be booze, it would be sugar. It would be baked goods.

I could pile whipped cream on a piece of pie!

I could slather it on bread pudding!

If I wanted whipped cream on a piece of cake that was thickly, richly, luxuriously frosted, I could do so!

I could do whatever I wanted!

I could order the chicken pot pie because I loved it so much, with that crust so flaky-smooth and delicious, that sauce so creamy and perfect. And two or three sides to go with it, which made sense, since the Rose & Emerald didn't clutter pot pies with vegetables. I could have a wonderful time ordering and then sitting there in a state of expectation. And thinking only of what I would eat. Like nothing else mattered.

I was *ravenous*.

But I would never get the chance to place my order.

Why would they change the program so that the award for Employee of the Year was announced and given out first thing, when every other year it didn't happen until nearly the end?

When the windows disappeared behind the drapes, and daylight was banished, the galaxy of lights in the banquet hall came on, each one shining palely, like round white faraway stars all over the ceiling. The executive who was playing the role of emcee this year was striding to the platform at the front, where the giant screen hung suspended.

The executive was the "mere formality" man I had the third interview with. He was miked up. His voice came booming through the hall, and why was he saying my name?

For a terrifying moment I was almost paralyzed, sitting there with my shoes off, my feet in nylon peds because I hadn't wanted to put on pantyhose. I'd recently shaved my legs, so I didn't have to worry about that, and why was the executive saying my name, really?

He was saying my name.

Just before the Rose & Emerald spotlight blasted my way, and the huge screen came shimmering to life to show a photo of a woman, and the woman was me, I glanced at the section of the hall where my department was. I saw what I hadn't wanted to acknowledge before. The table where the members of my team sat together was a table for ten. Counting me, the team numbered ten.

Ten were there.

Ten suit jackets, ten button-down shirts, ten neckties in perfect arrangements at ten throats.

Ten recent haircuts. Ten males together around a ten-person table.

Ten men.

Only one of them, somewhat younger than me, was not, or hadn't been, one of us. Right away I knew he hadn't joined them because he'd taken that seat number, randomly.

It was the way he sat there.

Newly belonging.

You can't work in companies for close to twenty years like I had, and not be able to read certain types of signals, signs. He was handsome in profile as I looked that way, healthy and fit and broad in the shoulders, and muscular but not too much, and at ease. He was looking quite fully relaxed, and pleased and glad about himself and all the world, and why would that be?

He was the man who got the position.

Who would be opening the box on the desk to take out his new computer.

Who would look out the window of that large cubicle, because a window was there.

Who would sit down in the chair at the desk right on top of the phantom of me. Like he was crushing a no one, a ghost no one knew was there.

I knew he was the one.

I just knew.

As it happened, two members of my department, both at the same time, met my eyes across the hall. They were the guys who shared a cubicle and were eager for me to leave mine, so one of them could take it.

Except for the new man, they were all turning my way. But those two looked at the new one and immediately back at me. Neither of them was any good at keeping anything hidden—they were still new enough to company life to lack skills for workplace poker faces. They lidded their eyes a little, looking downward, telling me that they were uncomfortable.

That's the new guy, they were signaling me. And nothing could be done about it!

And there was that photo. Larger than life. Huge. It was taken without my knowing. Like I'd been robbed of my own self.

This was the first time I'd seen it: me outdoors in the office park, approaching the entrance of our building, wearing jeans and the loose, bright-pink zip-up hoodie I'd grabbed from the trunk of my car that day for my regular walk. The day was very recent.

Meaning, the photo was taken *after* my experience with the man-boy in HR.

Was there a true Employee of the Year who'd been bumped, so they could give it to me instead? A sudden big change in the plan?

I couldn't know that, ever.

The hoodie in the photo was new. My kids' school had held a fundraiser, selling sweatshirts. In the photo, you couldn't see that the name of the school and their crest and logo were on the front, small and fairly discreet. The zipper was undone. The hoodie was wide open, like I was about to take it off, like I had worked up a sweat.

I looked sweaty. I looked like I was stressed and breathing hard.

That sweatshirt had come home to me with my kids the day before I went home to them and their father, and ate chili for dinner, and set my mouth and throat a little bit on fire, and my eyes watered up, and they didn't know about the promotion, and they didn't know I'd been over at the pond, crying.

The pink of the sweatshirt was very pink, like neon or a plastic outdoor flamingo. When I ordered that color, I thought it would be lighter, like a tea rose. But I didn't exchange it. Into my car it had gone, for cool days walking at work.

I could never know who took the photo. But I knew exactly when.

And suddenly the spotlight was blinding me.

Eighteen

I stood up. I didn't feel less tall than I'd felt in the high heels. I felt like my own self. I only had a couple of seconds to decide if I should sit down again and force my feet back into those shoes. How long would it have taken me to put them back on? A long time. Which I didn't have.

"Employee of the Year!" the executive was saying.

I knew this room by heart. I reminded myself I wasn't a stranger to the Rose & Emerald.

"Bye-bye," I said to the people at my table, even though I didn't know any of their names. They were clapping for me. So was everyone!

I didn't decide to be brave. It just happened.

It looked like I was heading for the front of the hall to join the executive who had uttered my name, like maybe I didn't understand how this was done. Like I was confused. Like I foolishly thought the announcement of my name was the summons to accept my award.

Like I'd never been to a banquet before and I didn't know the order, the protocol: lots of photos flashing by, remarks about me from fellow employees, a brief speech by my manager, and maybe a few words from the CEO or some other high-up who'd never met me or even waved hi in a hall, but would praise me and quote from things like evaluations, and my work history, and maybe the classes I took and how I performed in them, although probably, if he did, he wouldn't mention I paid the cost myself. He'd probably be vague about describing my results, with nice, easygoing words about what a fine woman I was, what a great sport, what a terrific team player. And so good about learning new things and improving myself!

I knew it seemed I was breaking the rules, as if I had an attitude problem.

That was a comment you never wanted to see on a yearly review. *She has an attitude problem.* I had worked so hard at being an employee with an attitude that was praiseworthy. But it must have seemed that, to me, becoming Employee of the Year meant I didn't have to care anymore about rules and decorum.

But I was determined to do what I was doing.

And just look at me.

The Employee of the Year was not supposed to hear her name and then barge up front breathlessly, in a hurry, head high, long in her strides, arms pumping the air.

This wasn't outside in the office park! This was indoors, with people at tables packed closely together!

The Employee of the Year could have bashed someone on the head with an elbow!

Or crashed into someone sitting innocently in a chair!

If the look on my face seemed to say I was happy, it was due to how good it felt to be on my own feet, not those heels. I wished, though, I wasn't practically barefoot.

I heard a smattering of laughter move in a wave through the hall from people who either felt nervous about me and my very wrong behavior, or saw me as overwhelmed, because of everyone in the company, from the highest paid to the lowest, I was the one singled out. I was the one being chosen for this award, the first-ever woman—and I was grateful and excited and thrilled, like I couldn't wait to get my hands on the official piece of paper that would serve as proof of my honor.

Up it was meant to go, my award, on a wall of my cubicle that had no door, no window.

And that was supposed to be that.

But on I kept going, the last thing anyone expected me to do, walking as fast as I could past the tables, past the executive, to the door that led out of the hall into a passageway you weren't supposed to enter unless you worked here.

A small crowd of Rose & Emerald waitstaffers had congregated by that corner, waiting to go around filling water glasses and taking orders from people who disobeyed the memo about ordering your meal through the online form the company wanted you to use.

You filled out the menu for the office who handled the banquet, and they'd be like, look how efficient we are! Look how organized! And meanwhile, were they forwarding data on what you'd be eating to HR? I'd heard it said that, yes, they did exactly that. No one had any way of getting evidence this actually happened. People in HR would never whistleblow or leak what they were up to.

I'd heard that private information such as your personal habits and your weight could end up in profiles of you that you never saw, because they were only available to bosses and HR people. Were these crazy conspiracy theories?

Maybe. Maybe not.

I'd also heard that some employees who ordered online did so as a cover. These in-the-know rebels ordered salads and plain slices of meat or poultry. When the waitstaff came around, they had the chance to say what they really wanted.

I might have done that very thing, if I hadn't decided to ignore the ordering form, because, on the day the form appeared in an email, I'd found out I had an excellent reason to decide *I wasn't attending the banquet.*

Why did I have to change my mind about that?

I could have been home. But no, I had to work out the calculation. If I didn't go, I would look like a coward. If only to myself.

And here I was, going straight toward the servers.

You knew who they were by the uniforms. Men and women alike wore black pants and satiny, loose tops resembling bowling shirts. This could have been a team at a bowling alley, and you'd wonder why their uniforms had no words, no name of the team or a sponsor.

Some shirts were red, with central panels of emerald green, on which red buttons were sewn with green thread. Or they were green with red panels, green buttons, red threads.

People who worked at the Rose & Emerald tended to stay on. It wasn't a high-turnover kind of place. These were employees who saw on a regular basis all sorts of things humans did, at all sorts of events, and also just going out for a meal or into the bar. It was not remarkable to them to realize a person attending a company banquet was *fleeing*.

They simply made room for me to barrel through. Someone opened the door into the narrow passage for me, and I said, "Thanks!"

Looking briefly back over my shoulder, I saw that the door had closed behind me. The Rose & Emerald people seemed worried I'd be pursued, and so what if I had no shoes on?

The door shut tightly to seal my escape. The waitstaff opted to take my side against anyone who might be after me.

I had allies.

Nineteen

The narrow corridor was not a connection with the kitchen. Nor did it lead to the bar. I'd never been inside the employees-only area, but I saw I might be able to get there, if I stuck to the course I was on.

I spotted a ladies' room a little way ahead, so I could finally deal with the fact that I hadn't peed for hours and hours.

They must have put up a full-length mirror for employees to check themselves head to toe before reporting for duty. I was alone in there. I didn't look at myself until after I emerged from one of the stalls.

There I was, me.

All of me: Trisha Donahue, Patricia Eileen Gilley Donahue, forty-four years old, not ungifted, not untalented, well educated, striver of betterments, actually an accomplisher of accomplishments, actually of sound mind, in good health, not unattractive, not dangerous to anyone in any way, basically a decent person, not too tall and not too short, not underweight or overweight, and overall lucky, lucky, lucky.

Exactly what was I luckiest about, this awful day, this wreck of a day?

I was luckiest about my light gray cotton cardigan with the inside pocket where my car keys were—my dress had no pockets. The sweater was loose enough to be a jacket, and therefore an excellent cover-up. I'd grabbed it and put it on at the last minute, hurrying my arms into the sleeves as I dashed out my front door.

I must have realized I'd made a mistake by reaching in my closet and grabbing a dress off a hanger. And, no big deal, whatever I grabbed would be my dress-up garment of the day. I'd gone for the part of the closet where my nonwork outfits were.

There was a light fixture inside. But no light bulb. How could I have taken out the old bulb, which obviously had burned out, and not replaced it? I must have been distracted on the way to a replacement.

I was always getting distracted. I was always multitasking.

Or, I had not been distracted or multitasking, and our household was out of bulbs when I needed a new one. We were always running out of things and it would feel impossible to keep up with list-making.

Things would often feel impossible.

I did not glance in a mirror before leaving home. I didn't even look down at myself.

The bedroom window shades had been closed. It was semi-dark as I got myself ready.

The dress I put on was suitable for a wedding, and thus fit the company's requirement of a banquet dress code. The only times I'd worn it were quite a few years earlier, during my pregnancies. There'd been lots of dressy social occasions during the months I was a human blimp, my breasts incredibly inflated, my belly a kettledrum.

My first son was bigger at birth than my second, but not by much. Both were giant babies. I'd been truly huge, and why was that dress even there, taking up closet space?

It was silk, expensive. The color was a soft orange-yellow, sort of like an apricot. I must have meant to have it altered, so I could wear it on my normal body.

It was several sizes too big for me now. The plunging round neckline, back when my chest was a bosom of overstuffed pillows, was situated fairly close to my neck. Now, the top front of the dress scooped down so low, a large portion of my bra would have been visible, had I not been lucky enough with my cover-up sweater, which, somehow, without realizing why, I'd buttoned all the way up. I was exposing no cleavage, no underwear.

So I stood there in the ladies' room and looked at the me in the mirror. I told myself that I didn't appear to be ridiculous. I didn't seem strangely comical, like a cartoon woman, or pitiful or odd in any way. I was just who I was. I could make myself smile, like I was taking my own photo.

"I love this sweater so much," I was saying. "I'm so lucky I put it on."

Back I went into the passageway. At the end was the door leading into the area of the Rose & Emerald for EMPLOYEES ONLY.

"Hey! Stop! You're not allowed in there! What's the matter with you? Can't you read?"

The voice was coming from the side of the passageway that shared a wall with outdoors. There, a door was propped open. In the sheen of sunlight filling the frame, no one was visible.

But then my eyes made out, on the stoop at the bottom of that frame, what appeared to be a strangely misshapen object about the size of a soccer ball—that is, a ball that once was round, but somehow, for some reason, became lumpish and pocked and distorted. The color was darkish gray.

It was a rock. That was the thing wedged in place to hold open the door.

And now that I'd noticed it, why did I feel that I couldn't pull myself away from staring at it? Like the rock had the power of taking hold of my attention completely. And then I wanted to squat down and touch it.

I forgot I wore no shoes. I forgot I looked like I'd put on a dress that didn't belong to me, like I'd grabbed it from a bin somewhere full of charitable donations.

I forgot that on my person I had no phone, no wallet, no money, no ID, no anything.

I even forgot that all I'd wanted to do was enter the section of the Rose & Emerald where I might be able to find someone who would help me. Someone who was not employed by my company.

"Oh my, I can't believe who it is," said the voice, which was alto-low, and warm and husky and throaty.

And there stepped inside from the doorway, from the light, as if coming toward me from some other dimension, a small and quite elderly woman I could swear I'd never seen before. She wore the same uniform as the waitstaffers in Big Hall, and over it was a boxy black utility vest with many pockets. Together with her black slacks, it looked like an informal suit. I remembered that this was the attire of people here who worked in the bar and the dining rooms that were not about large, special-menu events.

She was whitely pale, silver and white in her curly, downy hair, and lightly crinkled in her apple-round face. She wore no jewelry, no makeup. In height, she came up to my shoulders. She had to tip back her head to look at me and speak to me, but she was so deeply endowed with self-possession, she could make anyone realize that, when you talked down to her, you were only doing so literally, in a necessary physical way.

It seemed to me she would never allow herself to be talked down to in a superior way by someone who thinks it's cool to try making you feel they're important and you are not.

Something like that.

I made a mental note, like a command I could file in a readily available place, that I would follow her example, if only to help myself in my own mind.

I couldn't roll back time and return to an experience such as any time in my company when I was giving a presentation or explaining in a meeting a problem I had solved, and someone who understood absolutely zero of the subject would interrupt me, and either find fault with some tiny meaningless aspect of it, or repeat the meaning of what I'd said, in words of his own, like he was saying it better, and then everyone would nod and thank him!

And I would take a deep breath and feel myself shrinking inside, convinced for that moment I was incompetent, I was a phony, I did not deserve the job I had, I did not belong there.

Or that day in HR. When I had to meet with the man-boy, instead of someone senior. And the man-boy got up on an invisible high horse and talked down to me like I was a child.

And I could only be dazed and confused and shrunken. I could only drive away to the pond where the ducks were all gone. And cry.

I couldn't fix or change those situations. I could only look ahead.

I felt happy to be in this woman's presence, even though I hadn't a clue who she was.

She was saying, "Trisha! They told me a lady had a breakdown in the hall, and she was in trouble, and it's you. Trisha Gilley! I stepped out for a cigarette, and they buzzed me, and the lady turns out to be you. Well I never. Of all people!"

"I didn't have a breakdown," I said quickly.

She didn't seem to care what had happened, as if everything customers did, no matter how outlandish or pitiful or stupid, was all the same to her. She wasn't here to judge.

She didn't identify herself. Maybe it was impossible for her to imagine that anyone who met her could ever forget her, even if many years had gone by.

Who was she? Someone from my past. I didn't dare ask her to help me identify her.

I'd never seen her at other banquets. The fact that she recognized me was really surprising. I looked so different from the person "Trisha Gilley" used to be, I'd expect no one from my old life to recognize me at all.

"Well, let me tell you," she was saying, abruptly switching gears in our conversation. She pointed to her place of entrance. "That door can't be opened from outside. So excuse me a minute while I shut it, or there'll be hell to pay. Folks at functions like yours, when they block the rank and file from the bar, the rank and file will always try finding a way. Then they have to be caught and sent back into the hall."

"I wasn't trying to get to the bar," I said.

She smiled at me, gently and kindly.

"Of course you weren't, but no matter. We have to concentrate on taking care of what needs taking care of. I don't have much time, as I'm on my shift now, this being work time for me."

I was willing to offer my help in moving the rock out of the way. I wanted to put my hands on it. I didn't know why the desire came over me so strongly. I'd never seen one quite like it, although my experience with rocks was limited.

Why didn't I take even one geology course? Why did I know nothing about rocks? Why did I spend so much time improving myself as an employee of my company? Why had I never gone out into nature with my husband and children to look for interesting natural objects? Why didn't I make it a rule in my family that we had to have outdoor time just to be outdoors?

My kids never swam in water that wasn't a pool. They knew how to ice-skate, for hockey, but they had never skated on ice that was not in a rink indoors. The bikes they had were fat-tire dirt bikes, for tracks near their school we had to drive them to, and they never left the tracks. They had skateboards for the skate park we paid deluxe rates for, which meant joining other parents to rent that place a couple of times a month, so our kids didn't waste their skate time waiting in lines for their turns.

Our privileged, privileged kids.

They would look at me in amazement when I talked about what it was like to wander around my home territory freely, often aimlessly, from the time I came into possession of a bike. My husband would say, "Mom used to be wild." Our boys wouldn't think "wild" was something they'd like to try out for themselves. The thought of wandering around alone was sad to them, because it meant no one liked you enough to hang out with you, and you didn't have anywhere to go.

I'd feel I belonged to some other species.

And I would feel a little lonely.

I looked again at the rock propping open the door.

It didn't look too heavy for me to pick up. There was no stoop or stairway at the door. The jamb was level with the ground. I began to maneuver myself close enough to bend and lift it, but the woman reached it first, put her foot on it, and pushed against it until it rolled out of the frame.

And just before the door swung inward, and shut with a dull little thud, the voice of another, unseen person came in—a man's this time. He sounded old. He sounded like a male version of the woman beside me, who was taking hold of my arm and steering me the rest of the way down the hall, to the area of EMPLOYEES ONLY. Where I now seemed qualified to go.

The outside voice was loud, in a croaky, growly, old-man way. An admonishment was being shouted.

"For the last time, no more with the comet for a doorstop! And kicking it too! Cut it out with that!"

Twenty

A keypad was by the door for EMPLOYEES ONLY. The Rose & Emerald wasn't fooling around with privacy and security for staffers. The woman who was a stranger to me approached it to tap out the numbers of the passcode.

"Did that rock come from outer space, like, for real?"

You'd think I had not asked the question. She wanted to know, instead, if someone on duty in the banquet hall should retrieve my shoes for me, along with anything else I'd left behind. She seemed to take it for granted I would not be going back.

"Thank you for the offer, but I didn't leave anything else," I said. "I don't want my shoes. I'm done with them."

"Well then, I'm going to let you in."

"Wait, please. That man outdoors said *comet.*"

"He did no such thing."

"But I heard him."

"And so did I."

The woman's smile did not return. She held a gaze that told me she had zero tolerance for speaking to me about any subject she did not bring up herself. She didn't like being annoyed in this manner. She was running out of patience with me, and became even sterner in her expression. Yet I pushed.

"Do you keep the rock outdoors, like any rock?"

"That's a strange thing to ask," she said.

"I'm just curious. If I went outdoors, would I be able to see it?"

"See it? What *are* you talking about?"

"Actually, I'd like to touch it."

"Why?"

"I don't know," I said.

"But you saw it already. It's nothing but a stone. Stop bothering about it!"

"I'm not trying to be a bother."

"I've no time," she said. "Bye now, Trisha Gilley."

She was a master of mysteriousness, probably like all good, highly professional bartenders and waitstaffers. She could not have done a better job at cloaking herself in a cover of inscrutability, which also involved lying.

The word "comet" had been uttered!

Apparently, as an escapee from a large-group function, I had no rights in terms of information. Not even from someone who claimed to know me.

I was given a nudge inside that was almost a push, and then the woman backed away, letting the protected door close behind me. I hadn't expected her to retreat, leaving me there alone.

I found myself stepping into a sort of vestibule, or mini-lobby, which seemed to be a smaller version of the one with the fishbowl on a stand by Big Hall. But here, there wasn't a stand or a bowl. The walls on either side were lined with wooden shelves divided into individual spaces, like lockers without doors. Each had a printed sticker bearing not a name but a job title.

Quite a few were about waitstaffing and kitchen work. There were bussers, sous-chefs, dishwashers, sales, cooks, bar staff, sanitation, front of house, back office, maintenance, laundry, customer relations. All were equal in size and exactly alike. All these personal storage units, or cubbies, as my kids used to call such things in day care, were not issued or arranged according to orders of rank.

It really struck me that there was no hierarchy. "Head Chef," "Events Manager," and "Director of Operations" had the same sort of cubby as people who earned a paycheck cleaning toilets, scrubbing pots, removing stains on napkins and tablecloths, collecting and taking out trash, washing floors where a customer puked or spilled something.

In the cubbies were jackets, hats, sweaters, sweatshirts, folded-up changes of clothing for people who didn't arrive in their uniforms. And purses, backpacks, makeup bags, electric shavers, collapsible umbrellas, all kinds of personal items, unsecured, unlocked. Socks, too, here and there.

I had a flash of an idea: I could steal someone's shoes, then leave the Rose & Emerald.

Probably, I was thinking, people came to work in footwear not appropriate for work. Shoes perhaps in my size could have been placed underneath something else. It wouldn't have been stealing, not really. I would return anything I borrowed from a cubby.

How low could I sink?

If I succeeded in the robbery of someone's shoes, what could my next move be? Go up to the main road and start walking? Of course I couldn't consider hitchhiking—on the same road I once bike-traveled fearlessly. It would be just my luck to hop into a vehicle of a driver appearing to be kindly, friendly, helpful, and *wham*, I'd be hurt, I'd be killed.

If a murder took place, it would be my own fault, and what about my husband and my children? They'd be baffled at my funeral, and baffled all the rest of their lives. My kids would be saying, again and again, how they hadn't known I was attending the banquet. They hadn't even known the banquet was happening! They'd thought their mother was at work! My husband would be, why, why, why, and what was up with her own shoes not being worn?

Or, perhaps worse, someone from my company, maybe someone from my team, would come looking for me to drag me back into Big Hall, like a caveman in a cartoon I once saw. He held a club that was fashioned from some enormous animal bone, obviously to remind you of the ape in *2001: A Space Odyssey*, exactly like that. In the cartoon, he was dragging a semi-vertical cavewoman he had ambushed, had bashed unconscious, because the woman was totally fed up with what her life had become. Her only option was escaping, and at last, having worked up the courage, she tried to flee their lair. And there she was, being pulled along *by her hair,* and you're supposed to look at the drawing and read the caption and think, ha ha ha, this cartoon is so funny!

The caption said, "Good news! Couple reunited! Love conquers all!"

Once again, to my credit, I refused to let myself panic. I did not disturb the cubbies by riffling through people's possessions for the sake of my feet and also my appearance.

I was now beyond the vestibule-like area. Before, in all the times I'd come to the Rose & Emerald, I had no way of acquiring a clue as to what this section was all about. Or even that any such place was here. This was truly hidden territory. Not only was there no access for outsiders, you couldn't peer in from outside. There were no windows.

I'd thought, starting from the moment the old woman was tapping the code to the door, I would arrive at some sort of lounge or break room—some type of employee hangout place that would be normal, ordinary.

But no one was present. The deepening hush around me felt like a new friend, just for me. I didn't find it strange or alarming that I was the only person in a place where I was not supposed to be. By now, the different parts of the Rose & Emerald that were not banquet-related had opened for the day. People were at their jobs, cooking, taking calls, dealing with customers, cleaning something, filling water glasses, frosting a cake, going over invoices, ordering supplies, doing something wrong and doing it over, doing something right and being proud of it, fussing over something that needed fussing about. Or whatever they all were doing, in the complicated swarm of activity outside my newly found quiet.

A peacefulness entered all of my body, all of my mind. I was all right. I became aware that my brain was clicking back into its normal operational abilities, and was, in fact, working pretty well.

The employees' dining room also had no windows. It was not exactly a replica of Big Hall, like a much smaller banquet place, but it was close, in a way of its own.

Gathered here were half a dozen tables, some round, some square. They were bedraggled, lopsided castoffs, unsuitable for paying customers, including a pair of metal ones from the patio, which were dented and rusted and centered with holes for umbrella poles. The chairs, of the standard folding type, were wood, and looked injured or beat up, as if brought here for furniture-triage. These must have come from a supply closet where the Rose & Emerald stored seats for meetings and large events when more guests arrived than were listed.

So the furnishings were haphazard. All the tables were bare.

There should have been an air of desolation in here, I felt, a certain loneliness and tawdry sadness, like a distribution center for charitable items, where you have to get stuff you need, when you don't have anywhere else to go.

Yet nothing was bleak. Nothing felt depressing.

The walls were unadorned, but did not look drab or even empty. A paint job must have recently happened. The color was a pale, gentle yellow, the same as summer daylight when it was raining, but then the rain became a mild, fizzy mist.

Warmth was here, and not just in terms of temperature.

A lovely feel of being welcome was here. It was a safe zone.

The tables and chairs were in a state of waiting. Somehow, it was clear to me that sooner or later in this day, there'd be plates, silverware, glasses, noise, voices, dramas large and small, exhausted people, hungry people, smells of sweat, smells of bodies in uniforms that started out clean and were now far from it. And faint smells of laundry bleach if they brought in tablecloths and napkins. And good smells of good food.

Why didn't I ask that old woman to help me get something to eat? I could have gone after her instead of letting myself become all worked up about the rock. I didn't have to let her abandon me so easily. I could have been unconcerned about hurting her feelings by admitting she was a blank to me in terms of my past. I could have demanded to know how she knew me, the old me, Trisha Gilley. Or maybe not demanded—maybe asked her nicely.

I pulled out a chair at the table closest to me, a round one, oak, old, an antique, thick, smoothly polished, on a pedestal stand so rickety, the table tipped significantly when I leaned in and placed my arms on the surface. I sank down in myself a little, like any weary creature needing a rest.

I listened to the quiet. I had turned myself into a fugitive. It felt good.

Twenty-one

In that peaceable stillness, while my brain should have been trying to process what options I had for what to do next, I realized I'd had an encounter before with the man who was given my position.

I was delivered, from a memory file in a vault in my brain, a sharp, clear playback involving him.

At the time, he was a company man just starting out. He worked in a division far enough away from my section that it wasn't unusual we'd never met. There were overlaps in what we worked on, but we'd never intersected on any projects. If we had, he would have been pretty far junior to me.

I didn't know his name. Our one conversation was anonymous on his end, although he addressed me correctly, as Ms. Donahue.

I didn't ask him any questions about himself. I never had the chance. Plus, I didn't care. I wasn't being a hierarchy-snob. He presented himself as someone who believed in being respectful and polite, and *professional.* But he came up to me so closely, so almost intimately, the two of us could have been out at some bar, or some club where a band had been playing, and now it was time for hookups, and I was the stranger he chose to make a move on.

Something like that.

I was in the Starbucks at our office park, in line for takeout. He'd been leaving, with his, when he spotted me. As he walked to the exit, he made the decision to turn and approach me. He came up behind me, taking me by surprise.

Seemingly casually, he placed the hand that wasn't holding his coffee flat against my upper back, between my shoulders. He held it there lightly, not pressing against me, just flat-palming me, until I took a step sideways to shake him off. I gave him a look that meant, no way is that okay.

Or, absolutely do not do that again.

He was several years younger than me. I was guessing he might have coasted easily along paths in his life that would have been hard or impossible for others, even for other young, white, college-grad, heterosexual men who were not as good-looking, not as buff, not as skilled at being cloaked all over with a veneer this man probably thought of as *charm*, which was combined with being *a really super-great guy.* Perhaps many people, in his life so far, had agreed with him in his self-estimation. Perhaps he had fooled many he came in contact with.

"Hi, Ms. Donahue," he said.

Quite a few people were in front of me. The line was moving slowly. I couldn't go back to work without the one thing I needed just then. The espresso machine in my section had gone out of commission again, and I needed an afternoon jolt.

He said, "I'd love to buy you whatever you're ordering."

This was around the time our company was undergoing the regime change. Things at work were pretty chaotic. Unease was everywhere; tensions were high. The big shake-ups of people quitting outright had already happened, but ahead lay the various traumas of layoffs, firings, reductions in hours, new assignments.

For only a tiny while there was gossip that began in other departments and floated around our building as if someone had opened windows that were supposed to be sealed shut. Like fresh air was coming in, replacing the same old conditioning, the same old re-circulations.

The gossip was about, *Let's form a union!*

Which went nowhere.

Which ended quickly with those windows being locked.

As the daughter of people who used to be unionized in their workplace, and had to live through the ordeal of watching their union destroyed by new bosses, in another takeover, I could not have played the part of an objective bystander if people in my company made any progress in organizing. If "a union" turned out to be more than gossip. But I doubted I'd even be able to join one, given my rank and salary. I didn't know what I would have done to help.

I wasn't relieved when nothing came of it. Or maybe I was, and I just didn't want to feel awful by admitting that to myself.

One day, along with everyone else on my floor, I received a notice that I was required to go through a new assessment and review. It was all just routine, it was said, although nothing like this had ever happened before.

The new executives borrowed a large conference room in another building. You had to walk all the way across the office park to reach it. Directed there by people in HR, you entered a situation that you quickly discovered was similar to being a student and taking a standardized test, such as college boards.

Perhaps because I was someone who never had a bad experience with a test of any kind—unless I screwed it up on purpose, in the days when I was anti-school—I didn't mind what they were demanding. I took it in stride, as one more company thing to deal with.

In the borrowed room, surrounded by other test-takers, none of whom I knew, as they didn't let you go with your own department, I sat down at one of the long conference tables arranged in rows. There were dividers at every place, like portable mini-walls, boxing you in. I could not believe that HR or the new bosses spent time wondering if we would cheat on whatever this turned out to be.

But I had to be willing to go along with it.

At a small table up front, with a timer set up on a block of wood, there was a proctor from HR. This was a woman I'd run into now and then on my regular walks around the office park. She was a walker too. We used to greet each other cheerfully; she was about my age. Lately, her usual friendly expression had been absent. In the new regime, she took on a new, strict manner, and never smiled, as if she'd forgotten how.

She didn't say hi or even acknowledge me when I waved to her before settling down in my test-box.

Pens and the test form were already in place. The top page was for filling out your name, department, and the length of time you'd been with the company. And this: a statement to be signed, in which you promised *on your honor* you would not disclose the contents of the test to anyone in the company who had not yet taken it. If you failed to put your signature there, you were disqualified, as in, goodbye, we're putting you on a list of bad employees! If you broke what was essentially a nondisclosure agreement, there'd be some sort of not-stipulated penalty.

I signed it.

"You may begin," intoned the proctor.

The timer was a large round mechanical one, white with black numbers. When it began ticking, the sound of the clicks infiltrated the silence and took it over, tick tick tick tick tick, louder by the second. I didn't pay attention to how much time we were allowed. I just wanted to get it over with.

It was a personality assessment, sort of, with some random math problems and geography questions thrown in too: a bunch of pages of printed questions with empty spaces for answers.

How would you describe yourself in terms of colors? (List three colors and briefly state how each applies to you.)

What is 12.5% of $4,064.00?

If your department held a potluck lunch, what would you sign up to bring, and why?

On what continent is the city of Newcastle?

If the company were to offer employees free tickets to a concert, sporting event, or some other "night out on the town," what would be your preference?

On and on this thing went. There were about a hundred questions.

The first page contained a long, tedious set of instructions, which continued to the second. Twice in the set, once near the start and once again in the middle, as a reminder, you were advised to not begin working on the questions until you'd read all instructions carefully.

You were placed in the role of an idiot, more or less. I was reminded of a car I once had with a manual badly translated into English. "Do not shift to Park when vehicle continues in act of being driven! Do not operate vehicle while you are driver in driver seat in prone position!"

These instructions were not in bad English, but they were boring and seemed utterly unnecessary. They appeared custom-made to inspire you to skip them.

They were all about the importance of being truthful in your answers, of being thoughtful, of not simply writing down any old thing in order to beat the time clock, or giving an answer based on what you felt the company wanted you to say.

You were informed, very emphatically, that the length of time you took to complete the test would play a large part in your performance score.

At the conclusion of the instructions, in really small print, really easy to miss, it said that the next thing to do was turn to the last page and read the note at the bottom.

Which said: "STAND UP AND LEAVE THIS AREA. YOU HAVE COMPLETED THE TEST."

I postponed my departure, reluctant to be the first one out. I looked over the questions until I couldn't put it off any longer. When I rose at my place, I took a sweeping look around. Every other test-taker was writing answers. I saw that the timer still had quite a way to go.

It must have looked to everyone else that I'd given up, for some reason. The HR-woman proctor did not look up at me. I went back to my cubicle.

That night, I told my husband and kids all about it, at our dinner table. I also told them the test was a secret to employees who had yet to take it, and they were, Babe! Mom! We won't tell! We don't even know anyone you work with!

One of my husband's colleagues, in another time zone from us, had a conversation with him, one on one, after a tricky conference call. They talked about paperwork, about a form concerning some financial thing, which the colleague thought was stupid, not knowing that my husband was the one who created it. My husband grabbed the opportunity to resolve the conflict between them by telling him about the test. It was like, want to hear about a stupid form my wife told me about?

The colleague knew where I worked.

He was, as it happened, and unknown to my husband when he brought up the subject, the former college roommate and best friend of the father of the guy in the seat at the banquet that should have been mine, like the new position.

Who had not yet taken our company's test.

Who would take the test soon afterward and walk out of the borrowed room way ahead of the others in his group, perhaps in record time, like he had a gift for speed-reading, like he blazed through the instructions and rose in his own little triumph, and no one would ever know he was a cheater.

There he was in our Starbucks.

In my face.

His hand on me.

"I'd love to buy you whatever you're ordering."

Why he felt he should thank me for being the reason *he killed it with that test,* I had no idea. Or why he felt he needed to explain to me how he'd been tipped off about going straight to the final page. He sounded proud of himself. He felt he'd accomplished something he could boast about. If he hadn't been armed with insider information ahead of time, he'd still be in that room answering questions on the form, ha ha ha!

I turned down his offer. I stayed in line for my order. I thought about reporting him, but that only lasted one minute. Who would believe me? Who would find fault with me for talking about the test at home? Who would be quick to call me a liar, like I was trying to cast a bright young promising employee in a bad light?

It wasn't that I'd forgotten what happened until today. By the time I left Starbucks with my caffeine, the part of my brain that sequesters troubling knowledge had already kicked in, had already secured the knowledge in my personal vault. That particular file was not impossible to access, but doing so was extremely difficult.

In other words, until now, I blocked it out.

I must have seen him around our building, in our parking lot, plenty of times. Seen him without seeing him. He must have been rising all along in the company's ranks. I just hadn't paid attention.

From now on, I couldn't think fondly and longingly about the large cubicle with the window, the chair, the desk, the new computer, the phantom me. The glow was gone. That space from now on would be the place every day that housed someone proud to cheat.

Twenty-two

"Here. Try these and see if they fit. They were in our Lost and Found, for a really long time. But no one knows how they got there."

The teenage girl who came into the employees' dining room held out a pair of slip-on ankle boots, suede, dark brown, lined with fleece. They were scuffed and far from new, but perfectly wearable.

They were the most welcome, most wonderful things I'd ever been offered. I knew that my expression was conveying my surprise. And my pleasure. When I was around the age of this girl, sixteen or seventeen, this was the type of boot I looked at in shop windows, and on the feet of well-off girls in my high school. And couldn't afford to buy. And I'd get mad at myself for generating waves of self-pity I felt might never go away.

"Oh, thank you," I said.

They fit me, mostly. They were a little too big, but now my feet were happily shod. I was glad for the roominess, after those heels.

The girl's voice was light and gentle, like it sparkled. She was being nice to me at the same time she was sweetly ribbing me when she said, "They don't go so great with your dress, but you don't have lots of choices for anything that would."

"I hate this dress," I admitted. "But at least I sort of feel like Cinderella now."

"Then that would sort of make me your prince."

"Yes, it would," I said, beaming at her, not only because she seemed to have materialized at my side from out of nowhere to help me, but also because she was actually princely, in a feminine way, as if you took the story of Cinderella and combined those two characters into one.

She reminded me of some very young employees from other companies I'd seen around my office park, going about in pairs or groups. Their attire was corporate, in the sense they were keeping to dress codes. To me, they were living their last days of still being kids, although obviously they were newly out of college. Everything about them seemed to come from a sense of inner buoyancy. A personal liberty was inside them. You could tell it wasn't just about being young.

Or it wasn't just about office park employees in a state of being not-broken-in.

I'd wave hello and wonder about them. Were they boys? Were they girls? Did it matter? Maybe it didn't. I would experience some anxiety. I would feel like their mom. Could they keep on being unbreakable? Who was going to mess with them? Who had messed with them already?

This girl had a slender, taut, large-breasted body. She wore her Rose & Emerald uniform like it was a fashion statement. The standard black pants that were so ordinary on other members of the staff were, on her, stretchy yoga-type leggings going just below her knees. Where her elders favored the red and green, bowling-type shirts to fit loosely, hers was snug, and unbuttoned halfway down. Underneath was a tight black v-neck tank, and no bra, which made me feel I was learning a new lesson, or asking myself a new question. Why does anyone even bother wearing a bra?

Her long, black, glossy, beautiful hair was pulled back in a ponytail, but the top and sides were done in a buzz cut. The hairdo did not look weird on her. Or even daring. It just looked like, of course she would have this style, and the reason would be, she could look like a boy and a girl on her head.

I had the feeling she'd be okay about hanging around with me longer, so I could continue sitting there in the role of a grown-up appreciating her and sending vibes of approval. Probably she should have been in school. I couldn't help bringing that up.

I said, mom-like, "Why aren't you in school?"

"I am. Like, right now. They threw me out of real high school, so I got into an alternative one. They have programs where you get sent somewhere to learn stuff, like in the real world. This is where they put me."

"What are you learning?"

"Business management," said the girl, proudly. "I'm going to run something, some day. They put me in an office and they make me wear their uniform even though I'm not regular. But I don't have time to, like, talk. We have to get going. I need to hide you."

"Hide me?"

"You're kind of being looked for. What did you do?"

"It would take a long time to explain it," I said, sighing.

"That's what I always say about no more normal school for me. Do you want to be found?"

"I do not. I want to make a phone call, but I don't have my phone. I don't have any of my things with me."

She hesitated a moment, giving me a worried look.

"You might want to put off calling anyone, for a while," she said. "They're looking for you outside too. I mean, they're still having their banquet. But they've got, like, a posse. Nobody working here is helping them, so don't worry about that, okay?"

"Okay," I said, putting myself in her hands. "Can I give you some advice? For your future?"

"Sure!"

"Don't go to work in a corporation. Even if you think it'll just be for a little while."

She smiled at me brightly, cheerfully.

"Thanks, but I would never. Those people in there? In Big Hall? I looked at them! Boring, boring, boring. I feel *sorry* for them. Come on, let's go. Follow me!"

Twenty-three

A secret staircase led to the top floor of the Rose & Emerald.

Not much could be found about the background of this place. In a general wipeout of history, records were lost forever. A fire in a municipal building, sometime in the nineteen-sixties, destroyed all sorts of paperwork. An air of secrecy, of privacy, along with an aversion to publicity, seemed to have always surrounded this place, enhancing it even more.

What there was, was the stuff of handed-down stories, fables, myths.

It was part of a farm. It was the home of a wealthy family whose money came from ownership of factories, but nothing remained of them. It was a rehab hospital for wounded soldiers, an inn for wealthy city people to escape to, a venue for ballroom dancing with big swing bands, a place to rent out to carnivals, circuses, political meetings, and religious organizations conducting revivals, conventions, retreats. And those were only the tales I'd heard about. At one time or another in the past, the building and grounds held something of everything, it would seem, like a movie studio, or a computer you can empty of programs to make way for new ones.

No one had ever written an account of this area, or of people connected to the original construction and ownership. It was the same as if the Rose & Emerald had decided on its own, like a living, intelligent organism, to exist outside of history. Not all of the stories could be true.

But that's how you get to roll when you're a place that's legendary.

When I was planning my wedding and wanted it to be here, I learned from my husband-to-be that members of his family went poking around in newspaper and library archives. He thought it was funny that they hoped to discover a horrible event that would be potent enough to cast a bag of bad omens not only for that day, but for the rest of our lives.

They thought that because I grew up so not-well-off, so not-like-them, I'd be naturally superstitious. Like I could be given evidence of a murder on the premises, or any other terrible scandal, and I'd react by deciding the Rose & Emerald was the last place on the earth I'd want to go, ever, for any reason at all.

But they didn't find anything they could use. Not even one little tale of a crime, or a room that was haunted by some long-ago villain with malicious, unfinished business to attend to.

My husband still liked to laugh about that. Babe! My family was looking for ghosts! Imagine anyone thinking you're superstitious! Any ghost would be afraid of *you*!

And now, in my newly booted feet, with my new sense of liberation, which was still a little shaky, I followed my guide as she led me up dim, narrow, steep stairs. There was no landing for access to the second floor. This was a direct route to the attic area extending through the whole building.

At each step, I was aware that I was climbing a well-trodden path, as if my sight had been boosted, somehow. I could make out the imprints of footsteps embedded here long before there was any such person in the world as me. The air wasn't dusty or musty, just old, just shut off from outdoor freshness, as in any window-less shaft. The electric wall fixtures giving faint yellowish light could have been the same sconces that once held gaslight, or even candles.

I was light-headed and stomach-rumbly from the breakfast I never had and the lunch I wasn't getting, but I didn't care. I was starting to feel excited, like I was an explorer.

I thought I'd enter an actual attic, filled with antiques and trunks of stuff to rummage in, and memorabilia from the days when I was a girl sneaking around this place, loving this place.

I felt I'd be glad to wait out my company's banquet practically a whole galaxy away from what I had fled. Thanks to my rescuer, I'd be hiding in a private world of stuff that regular customers never had the chance to see, like I had earned the right to be a Rose & Emerald insider.

I could not remember the last time my heart quickened like this, with a happy, buoyant expectation—and then my guide pushed open a door so low we both had to duck to pass through.

I entered a loft filled with offices.

I walked into cubicles.

We were up in the rafters, on a floor of uncovered boards, in the geometry of low walls and exposed beams that under-sided the roof.

Whoever designed the layout of the various work spaces did a good job at giving whoever came here a sense of not being cramped, not being oppressed. It would have been nice to have skylights. But the lamps and mounted globes were a decent replacement for light of day. By the windows, there was no furniture. No cubicles. Just open spaces and natural light and the summery air coming in on little breezes.

No one here would have to compete for the privilege of a seat all day where you could look at the sky, the season, the world outside.

The three-quarter cubicle walls were like sturdy screens, and as brightly colored as if they came from a LEGO set: red, yellow, green, blue, orange. These did not give an impression of being meant for kids. They looked chosen for grown-ups who might appreciate colors, seeing as how their jobs took place in an attic.

Each cubicle had for a desk a simple table and cushiony chair of the type sold inexpensively at discount office stores. There were electrical outlets but nothing was plugged in. The desks were bare, with low file cabinets at either end. They looked new. Everything looked new, and smelled new—very, very brand new, as if taken out of wrappings or packing boxes quite recently.

Portable pole fans whirred softly here and there on their stands. I listened to their movements in the stillness. I listened to the sounds of breeze-rustling leaves in the high old trees nearby. The hush I had felt beside me as a friend, in the secret dining room, had mounted the dim stairs with me. It seemed to take on more depth, and more layers, as if the peaceable quiet had the power of growing.

No one was here except me and my guide, who could see that I was so curious, I was standing there dumbfounded. Did she help me out with an explanation?

She did not.

I asked her, "What's all this for?"

"It's new," she said.

"But what will happen here?"

"I told you before. They take people for programs and stuff."

"But what for?"

"Oh, you know, stuff."

"Like for education?"

"You know what? I have to get downstairs to the office they put me in," she said. "I have, like, a ton of things to do today. They're scared I'll screw up like I'm a juvenile delinquent. Which I'm not! Bye! Nice meeting you!"

"Hold on a minute," I said. "Please tell me what I'm supposed to do up here."

"Be okay! Be safe! Which you are!"

Without another word, my guide, my princess-prince, my Rose & Emerald rescuer, turned abruptly, swinging her ponytail like the flutter of a goodbye-wave. She ducked through the doorway, gently closed the door behind her, and abandoned me.

Now I was agitated.

The last thing I felt like doing was sitting down at a tabletop desk in a cubicle, and anyway, I would never be able to choose which wall color. Or I'd choose a color and probably within minutes I'd stop liking it. I would have to switch to another, and the same thing would happen. I'd be playing musical chairs with myself, like Goldilocks in the home of the bears, an actual grown-up, weirded-out Goldilocks, and what about my new sense of liberation?

What liberation?

Who was I kidding?

I was a company woman. At the end of the banquet, I'd still be Employee of the Year. I'd still be reeling from getting kicked in the head because, yes, I'd had a very big expectation. I had contained in myself a reservoir of good faith—of believing things would go fairly for me. Because why wouldn't the promotion be mine?

Into the company newsletter, onto the company's website, posted on the company's Facebook, tweeted on the company's Twitter, and proclaimed who knew where else, would be the news that Trisha Donahue was their first-ever woman to be Employee of the Year.

Like I was so special.

Like no other woman in the company, presently or before me, was anywhere near as outstanding as I was.

And what about an honorarium to go with the honor? Would I be given a check? Would it go into my bank account as a direct deposit?

I was a special and outstanding woman for free!

I felt the wet heat of my own steam escaping from every pore of my skin. I really was like that super-whistling kettle in my department's little kitchen. At least I wasn't screaming.

But I didn't want to boil inside myself. I didn't want to wreck this peace. Maybe I could have helped my own turbulence by deciding, oh, it's only a job. You go to work, you earn your paycheck, you put up with things.

But it wasn't only a job.

I stepped into the nearest cubicle and seized a chair. I dragged it to a window with a view of the mountain, where low, fat, puffy white clouds seemed to leave the sky and settle all over the top, like mounds and mounds of whipped cream.

Why didn't I know anything about painting a picture? I felt I'd never looked at anything before that made me wish I could paint.

It was a strange new sensation. A whole new emotion. A whole new sense of "I want" and "I wish."

And then I remembered Olaf.

I remembered getting in trouble long ago, in the eighth grade, in English class, when we had to memorize a poem by an American, and stand and deliver it.

I picked e.e. cummings. So did the very popular girl whose friend I was not. But we chose different poems.

She did a lovely job reciting "somewhere i have never travelled, gladly beyond." I remembered the hush enfolding us all, like a spell we were under, like a necessary, wonderful accompaniment. Her voice sounded harp-like musical as she spoke of frail gestures, petals, a rose. When she reached the part about the heart of a flower shutting down because of *snow carefully everywhere descending,* it was amazing to look out the window and see there wasn't any snow.

Soon it was my turn. I got up. My choice was "i sing of Olaf glad and big."

Learning that poem was the first time I applied myself to the thing called "learning." I was still a long way from buckling down and setting my sights on college, the outside world, moving on, moving up. But something about Olaf got to me. I hadn't known anything about war, what war even is, besides facts to remember so I could pass a test. I certainly hadn't known what a conscientious objector is.

I did some research. I went to a library. I gathered up data. I liked it!

Of course the teacher knew what was coming in that poem, about Olaf declaring what he wouldn't kiss, and then what was coming afterward. I was stopped before I could utter *your fucking flag.*

I was told to skip that line. I'd eagerly looked forward to saying it, but I didn't want to get a failing grade, not with all the work I'd put in. So I felt I needed to be compliant. I would raise no objection. I would be practical.

But then, when I knew I was about to be shut up again, I paused.

I had come to the line where Olaf is saying the words of what I considered the most perfect line ever written in the world.

I interrupted myself with about twenty seconds of silence. In a moment of unexpected thirteen-year-old awareness, it dawned on me that in all the time I'd spent with that poem, I just then realized the fact that the only words with capital letters were God, Olaf, and Christ.

I could see the lines in printed form scrolling through my brain, with those three capitals bold, magnified.

But I didn't ever say what I had discovered. I didn't want to draw that kind of attention to myself. Or be laughed at for being serious.

Yet I had to honor Olaf. Why should I not honor Olaf when he was in the same league as God and Christ? And he was *cool.* That was my reasoning. I stood my ground. I defied the order to censor myself. I straightened my back and held my head high and spoke what needed to be said. I put an emphasis on the second word, as I felt that was the way the poet intended it.

"There is some shit I will not eat."

I was thrown out of class, but I didn't get expelled. I had to memorize a poem the teacher picked. I have no memory of what it was. Something long and sentimental and boring. I kept thinking of Olaf the whole time. I conducted private conversations with him, like he existed only as ears. I would tell him that if I were him, I'd do the same fucking thing. I would try to have his same kind of courage. I would eat no shit.

"Olaf."

I found myself saying that name, sitting high among treetops by a Rose & Emerald window. I watched in stillness as another white cloud drifted downward, as if dropping away from the sky, and I wondered, what happened to me?

Twenty-four

Food!

And I knew the person bringing lunch to me, in a Rose & Emerald uniform.

"Hi, Trish. How's it going?"

You'd think we last saw each other a day ago, when I hadn't laid eyes on him for over a quarter of a century.

Turk, he was called. When I knew him, he was lean to the point of being almost too skinny, and he was sharp and keen in his beautiful big brown eyes that could glint sometimes with the light of being smart and trustworthy, and wary and edgy, all at once.

If he'd gone to the trouble of playing an instrument, I used to think, he could have been a rock star. He had a standoffish manner easily taken for arrogance, but not in an adolescent way. It didn't matter to him that he was a teenager. He'd been a man since he was, like, eleven, he'd say, and you'd believe him, although he barely had to shave, and his voice would crack now and then into the voice of a little boy.

He was "Turk" because once on a dare when he was high on pot with his friends, he walked into a supermarket, ordered a deli rotisserie chicken, managed to get it into his backpack, and strolled out. It helped that it was late in the evening and there were not many grown-ups among the employees.

The chicken was quite large. The members of his boy gang were so stoned, they thought they were eating a turkey. At the time, it was almost Thanksgiving.

That was my favorite story about him, as disgusted as I was to think of those guys ripping apart cooked poultry in the woods behind the same grocery store, like apes, like they couldn't even wait to proceed to someone's kitchen. I knew he wasn't basically a thief. I knew he was scared he'd be caught. He was forever trying to prove himself. His own sense of worth or something. His manliness.

He was brilliant at pretending he wasn't growing up in what to me was luxury. I was never in his house. It was an ordinary large colonial, but to my eyes it was a mansion. His bedroom, I knew, had its own bathroom. I couldn't imagine what that might be like. He never owned just one pair of shoes at a time. I couldn't imagine that either.

His family had something to do with commercial real estate. He was supposed to be part of it. He took shop. He talked about trades. He was going to become an electrician, a mason, a carpenter; it changed weekly. He sat in the back in every class and acted like he was deaf and mute if a teacher called on him. He got away with what he called his "resistance," when kids who were modeling themselves on him kept getting detentions.

He dressed grunge. He claimed he hadn't spoken a word to his parents since he was a toddler just emerging from babbling, and you believed that too. He had the idea he'd been adopted. He did not believe his own birth certificate.

I wanted to be in love with him, but I wasn't.

We never called each other boyfriend and girlfriend, yet he was the closest to a boyfriend I'd ever had. We never made love. Just almost. We'd go for it, all grabby and heated, but it just kept fizzling out. Or one of us, or both of us, would be too high. Or too cold, as it was always outdoors in his favorite hiding place, in a grove of willows near a cemetery.

We loved cemeteries, we'd declare to each other. The dead won't rise up and tell us what to do!

We talked. We went riding around in the red vw Bug he inherited from an older sister. When he lost his license after his third cop-stop for driving under the influence—although never with me—we spent hours alone walking and smoking dope and talking and talking.

All along, he never knew the first real thing about me. It wasn't his fault. I was kind of secretive. I was a pretender too. He thought I never handed in homework, never scored above average on a test, never read a book.

Our regional high school was gigantic. The first thing you learned was how easy it could be to keep yourself in the background. I was rarely in classes with anyone I hung out with. By the time I could see graduation on the horizon, like a sighting of land on a boat you expected to be on sea waves forever, I was willing to admit to myself I'd found some freedom. The way the school worked was perfect for me. I could map my own way. And keep quiet about it.

Turk's family moved away somewhere, around the time I was nineteen. I wasn't proud of the fact I never went looking for him, or anyone else, on my visits home to see my parents. Those didn't happen very often. I was busy. I was turning into someone else.

Turk. The last thing he said to me was that he'd only found out he had a heart on the day I broke it. I was leaving for college? I was saying goodbye? I got into a college? What was *wrong* with me?

"Hi, Turk," I said. "I'm okay, but things aren't going so great for me today. You probably already knew that. You *work* here?"

"Yeah. The uniform, right? A giveaway. You're married?"

"I am."

"Kids?"

"Two. Boys."

"Sweet," he said. "They, like, healthy and everything?"

"I'm lucky, yes. What about you?"

"I brought you something to eat."

In his hands was a Rose & Emerald dinner plate with a silver lid. He lifted the lid with a solemn little flourish of drama.

I said, "Wow, are you a waiter?"

"Yeah."

Instead of giving me the plate right away, he looked around at the cubicles with their colored walls. He chose the orange one. I followed him, bypassing a green and a blue, and I realized he remembered that orange was my favorite color when I was in high school. I remembered a gorgeous autumn day in almost-twilight when he still could legally drive.

We tooled around back roads for a while, then he pulled to a stop at the edge of a field full of pumpkins close to ready for picking.

He had rolled a joint but we didn't smoke it. The trees around us were brilliant with fiery, orange leaves. The orange pumpkins were as big as orange moons. To the west, sunset streaked the horizon with glimmering shades of orange that seemed to ripple and shimmer, as if putting on a show for us.

I had felt I was existing, for just a few moments, in a world where it was possible to feel joy.

You never forget your first time ever of joy, I realized. You can misplace those moments in a memory vault, like a folder wrongly filed, but your first time will always be there. It can never stop being brand new. It can never stop being the best.

I learned joy because of you, I wasn't saying to Turk.

He had set my plate on the desk. He produced from a pocket of his Rose & Emerald shirt a set of tableware wrapped in a linen napkin, white and thin and worn and a little flimsy, like all the napkins here.

"You don't have to tip me," he said.

I smiled back at his smile. He still had that thing he did with his mouth, a lopsided grin, goofy, kissable.

Oh no! All these years gone by, and I wanted to kiss him?

"I can't tip you. I don't have my bag. Or my wallet, or anything. I forgot all my stuff in my car, back where I work."

"I heard you're not carrying anything around with you. I'm sorry I didn't bring you anything to drink. I just thought of that now. It's busy downstairs, what with regular people and your, you know, company. Your banquet."

"You're not working it?"

"I never do events," he said, without elaborating.

He placed the napkin next to the plate, the silverware on top of the napkin. He stood by, sort of at attention, while I took my seat at what was now my lunch table. He might have had a phone on his person. In a pocket.

Which he could reach into. Lending me his phone, he could have made it happen that I called my husband. *Come get me.*

Turk wore no wedding ring. I looked. I saw what appeared to be a half circle of indentation and paler skin. It didn't seem he took his ring off to do his waitering. That mark looked like it had been there quite a while. I was seeing it in the act of fading.

I didn't ask about it. He'd already let me know he wasn't open to giving me that kind of information. I needed to get a grip on myself, on account of what was physically stirring inside me, underneath my sweater, my ridiculous too-big dress, my bra I'd already wished I wasn't wearing, my skin head to toe, my under-pants, *oh no!*

I didn't need my body to be remembering going all creamy between my thighs sometimes when he and I almost fucked and then we didn't.

You do not pick up where you left off with an old boyfriend you never ever actually called your boyfriend!

The whole time I was a married woman with a career, especially after I became a mom, I never could figure out how anyone found the time to commit adultery. Certainly not anyone like me, with the schedule I had, the demands on me meshed into the fabric of my life. Every other minute at work I was hearing some new bit of gossip about so-and-so having an affair, so-and-so being seen in some hotel, some bar far removed from their regular territory. If the so-and-so was a parent working full-time, I'd think, no way! Like I'd been told the plot of a movie.

I was so naive about that.

There could be time! Time didn't have to be a strict, immutable thing! Time could be elastic, malleable, open!

"I hope you didn't become a vegetarian," said Turk.

"I totally didn't."

"Well, you should eat. You shouldn't let this get cold."

The meal he brought me was not from the menu for banquets. The grilled salmon steak was juiced with lime and buttery-glazed with specks of cilantro. The long, slender, very green beans had been sautéed with pecans and bits of bacon. The two halves of the twice-baked potato were loaded with I didn't know how many different kinds of cheese, and also bits of mushrooms first cooked in butter and wine.

I didn't know what to say. I had so many questions to ask him.

"Thank you," I said.

He was a profoundly handsome man. Maybe not in a conventional sense, but in his own way. His edgy bravado was a calmness now, his adolescent skinniness a grown-up, attractive geometry of slimness, even in that baggy shirt. He had some tiny creases around his eyes, but he still had his same old eyes, set a little more deeply.

We were the same age. I knew I looked forty-four, and probably, today, at least several years older. Turk looked maybe thirty. He looked to me like he'd be young forever.

What if I held out my hand to his? What if I gave him my number?

Not my cell though. My husband and kids loved to get hold of my phone, not to spy on me, or poke around to find out what I had stored there, but to try cracking whatever new passcode I'd set. Sometimes I made it easy for them, just to see the three of them turn jubilant, having outfoxed me.

But what about my work phone? Or my work email?

Then I heard the muted sound of beeping. He had a pager in some pocket.

"Duty calls," he said.

I ignored that. "I can't believe I'm seeing you," I said.

His eyes met mine. Finally. He'd been avoiding directness.

"Did you think I was dead, Trish?"

"Dead?"

"You must've heard about my, you know, trips to rehab."

"Rehab?"

"Don't ask. A lot of different times. It's past, all that. I'm good now."

"You look pretty good, Turk."

He did not say the same to me. I couldn't tell if he was struggling in himself to pretend he was only my waiter.

Was it about booze? Drugs? Both?

"I'm in a decent place. A kind of halfway house," he said.

"Can I . . ."

He cut me off, shaking his head. He saw the direction I was heading, probably as soon as I knew it myself. I couldn't tell if he thought I'd be leading us into dangerous territory, or if he bore me too much of a grudge that would always be there.

"Listen, Trish. I'm not telling you where I live, or anything. You can't ever try to contact me."

"What if I come back here someday? We could talk."

"I'm almost done with my job here. I've got another one lined up."

"What about today, before I go home?"

"Trish?"

"What?"

"I have to go."

"Can I ask you one more thing?"

I didn't wait for him to answer yes or no.

I said, "Did you volunteer to bring me my lunch? I figure someone down there decided to feed me. To be nice to me. To help me. So, did you volunteer to come up here, or did you get assigned?"

"I volunteered. I saw you get up and run out of Big Hall."

"But you weren't in there."

"Trish. Cameras? Monitors? You think they wouldn't keep track of an event? You looked like the star in a show."

"I did?"

"Yeah," he said.

I did not hold out my hand to him. I knew I wouldn't be able to bear it if he refused me even the slightest touch.

I wouldn't be able to bear it even more if we skin-grazed each other, and then our fingers would interlock, gladly, comfortably, naturally, the way they used to, him at the wheel of his Bug, him beside me looking at graves in that cemetery, him in front of me when I said I was clearing out, not saying I was sorry I hurt him, and he took hold of my hands and gripped me hard, really hard, making it a struggle for me to pull free. I remembered I'd been a little afraid of him.

"Enjoy your lunch," he said.

And now those words would be his last to me ever.

Twenty-five

I met my husband in the slow, maddening crawl of a jam resulting from a highway accident several miles away. He was directing traffic. When I approached the figure of him standing there, I thought he was a cop in civilian clothes who knew what he was doing, like he'd been in the area anyway, on a day off.

The first thing I noticed was what a great time he was having.

He wasn't jolly and dramatic and attention-seeking, with behaviors you can see sometimes in traffic people so worn down and bored with their job, they have to put on a performance just to get through their shift without feeling they're turning into zombies. And the traffic jam worsens because drivers are taking out phones to make videos.

It wasn't like that. This controller of car-flow appeared to be a man in his element, raising and lowering his arms, lifting a hand palm up, with simple, natural grace.

Yes, grace. That was the word I'd thought of.

You'd think that instead of ordering you to *stop your car right now or I'll ticket you or even pull out my gun,* he was offering some excellent advice, like giving you a gift of the very thing you needed.

I wasn't being delusional on account of the state I was in that day. He made a phenomenal first impression on me.

It was summer, sweaty and scorched-air hot, the kind of day when it was unbelievable we were close to the coast. The Atlantic with its cool salty winds could have dried up, as if the scanty breezes were coming our way from a desert. The time was close to six, post-work, with no hope of relief in night darkness. Given what the summer had been like so far, the night would probably be even hotter. The used Honda I'd recently bought, my first car ever, came with perfect air-conditioning that lasted about one week. I couldn't afford to get it fixed.

I was perspiring like crazy. I was miserable. I had no friends. Everyone I knew in college had scattered, and talking on the phone and sending emails didn't make up for not being together anymore. I wasn't lonely, not really, not like where it hurts so much you feel physically sick. But I was close to that.

This was when I worked in my first company. The office park where it was located wasn't far from a large shopping mall situated just off the highway. The mall had given some of its parking lot to a bunch of trailer trucks bearing swimming pools set up on flatbeds. A firehouse had sent over a water tank on wheels.

It was sort of a carnival, extremely popular. Even without the accident, the traffic would have been a nightmare. Somehow, a pool truck leaving the mall, with the pool still full of water, rammed into an open-bed pickup in which the driver was transporting tomatoes, in crates that had no lids.

A flood took place when the pool no longer contained its water. Most likely, the number of tomatoes remaining in the pickup was zero. A minor disaster of a mess had been created.

A long, narrow driveway was the only way for me to reach the access road that was the only way to the highway. That road was bumper-to-bumper packed. At the spot where the driveway met the road was the man I would marry.

I stopped thinking he was a cop when I came nearer and noticed the laminated identification card dangling at his hip. He had clipped it to a belt loop. He had shorts on, dark green Bermuda shorts, going exactly to the tops of his knees. And a tucked-in white shirt you could tell he'd worn with a suit jacket. The sleeves were rolled up to his elbows. From the way the shirt was clinging to him, so damply, I saw he wore no undershirt.

Most men in my workplace wore them all the time, some like T-shirts, some tanks. My company at the time had a cafeteria, not with offerings of cooked meals, but with microwaves and vending machines for sandwiches and disposable bowls of salad, soup, and dehydrated mystery something or other never tasting like real food.

At the table I'd joined, all women, we could have a good time complaining about what we were eating, as if we never brought in our own lunches for this purpose. It was similar to a bonding experience. It was the one thing in my life allowing me to not be lonely like I was sick.

We were a random group of people, not always the same. You could join or not on any given day. Our jobs were varied. A manager could be sitting beside a marketing trainee, an administrative assistant beside a finance specialist, a data clerk receiving minimum wage beside someone such as myself with a storehouse of education and a big supply of geeky know-how. We had little in common. We were multiracial, straight and gay, parents and not, physical workout regulars and those who could not believe such a thing exists as a workstation attached to a treadmill.

One of the women was an expert at predicting if a guy was a T-shirt wearer or a tank. Whenever she made a guess, someone would have to find out. When a new guy appeared, it would be time to place bets involving coins and dollars for the machines.

So, "not a cop" and "no undershirt" became two of the data points I first acquired about the mysterious director of traffic.

I recognized the company that issued the ID at his waistline where no belt was. I couldn't help wondering, under those shorts, was he in boxers or briefs? We speculated about that too at our lunch table, making guesses from the way a guy walked by, took his seat, banged at a machine that wasn't properly dispensing. We asked each other, if one of us went up to a guy and made an effort to know his type of underwear, would he accuse us of sexual harassment? Then that would be the funniest thing ever, even though we knew it wasn't funny at all.

Inching my car forward, I let the thought cross my mind that the not-a-cop guy might be wearing no underwear. I imagined his shorts becoming too loose at the waist and slipping down.

I had shocked myself! But it was a really nice shock.

Basically, the various buildings in the office park were alike. But one stood apart, as a multistory house stands so differently in a neighborhood of ranches. It wasn't a company I'd applied to. They were all about moving things around globally—money, goods, people, animals, whatever. They were like a frat house among dorms. It never occurred to me that this man was on track for account management, or on any track at all.

Total slacker level, I thought. I would find out later that if you showed up at his workplace in anything other than a regular suit, you weren't sent home like with a dress code in school, but you were fined. You were paycheck-docked.

The molecule in this man of being a tiny bit inclined to independence was really speaking to me.

His self-appointed job was to stop the flow of traffic in the access road to allow vehicles from the office park to exit and join the jam. My windows were open, rare among the cars that were functioning coolly. My radio was set on scan. He heard music playing faintly from the time I'd been several vehicles back.

The one with the music. That was me. Like an ID to him.

Then my turn for the access road arrived.

He leaned toward me. I looked at him. He looked at me.

He said, "Please hit that one, okay?"

I hadn't been stopping the scan. The roll-by of static and music and talking had been giving me a comforting level of background noise, helping me bear the now and then blasts of honking horns.

The piece he asked me to let play was "Free Fallin'." The Tom Petty version, of his own song.

I tapped the knob. I might have let it play on my own if I hadn't been in a mood where something so aching, so true-sounding, so very sad, might have caused me to burst into tears—that is, if I'd heard it all alone.

He said, "Could you turn it up?"

"I can't. This is as loud as it goes. It's a piece of junk radio."

"Bummer."

"I know."

His face and neck were dripping beads of sweat. Later we would say how cool it was that the first time we saw each other, we were wet.

Fortunately for the long line of cars behind me, the song was near the end. I believed he would have held me there, had it only just started.

"Great song," he said.

I agreed. "I love Tom Petty," I said. "But Stevie Nicks does it better."

His face went animated with a sudden soft glee.

"Unbelievable! I was just about to say the same thing! She *slays* me. By the way, you wouldn't happen to have a towel or something in there, would you?"

I could see he'd forgotten what he'd been doing, and why he was standing there. I didn't want to drive away from him. He wanted me to stay. I didn't know how I realized that, but I did.

Looking at him, talking to him, felt like two of the most natural things I'd ever experienced. Why didn't I have a towel in my car? Why couldn't I hand him a towel he'd have to return to me?

Someone back in the queue I was in decided it was important to shout at us to cut it out with the socializing. Obscenities were uttered. Threats.

The not-a-cop did not seem perturbed.

"I never directed traffic before," he confessed.

"You're doing a pretty good job."

"Well, I stepped up."

"I can see that."

"I guess I'd better let you out of here."

He moved away and made it happen that a space was open to me in the access road. You can't feel the wrenching ache of a parting with someone you just met, so I told myself that what I felt was only because of Tom Petty.

I turned off the radio, to not hear any other songs. I wanted that one to linger.

It took me over two hours to make the eight-mile trip to the apartment where I'd recently moved. I drove through some puddles on the highway of pulpy tomato soup. I might have thought about him the whole way if I didn't have to worry about freaking out because my engine overheated. Which it didn't.

Then I couldn't get him out of my mind.

His company didn't have a lobby with a receptionist, not that I could stride in there and ask to be put in touch with him. But maybe I could describe him. He wears Bermudas? He's kind of a laid-back guy, easy to talk to?

I hadn't counted on the fact he'd met my car as well as me.

When I was leaving work the next day, I found on my windshield a leaf from one of the nearby trees, as if it had fallen, as if this were autumn. The bottom of the stem was tucked in a wiper blade. He had written in black Sharpie on the leaf's underside. His phone number and three words.

"Shorts guy. Hoping."

I'd wanted to save the leaf, after I called him. Which I did there and then. But stupidly, I put it on my dashboard. It blew away, out the window. I couldn't stop on the highway to retrieve it.

He would tell me the next time we talked that he had destroyed half a dozen leaves by bearing down too hard with the Sharpie and tearing them.

He didn't know how he'd come up with the idea. It was a whole new thing for him. He couldn't remember any other time in his life a leaf was in his hands. What you did with leaves that were not attached to trees was hire landscapers to arrive with a blower and blow them away from your lawn.

It had felt weird to find himself looking around his office for a Sharpie. He'd had to borrow one from the administrative assistant who handled schedules for trips and meetings. She was forever writing reminders on sticky notes.

Did I think it was dumb thing to do?

I didn't think it was dumb. I had to say so maybe one hundred times before he'd believe me.

After the first time we made love, he recited a list of verbs, like an impromptu language exercise. He wanted to let me know the things he knew how to do—the extracurricular things he'd taken lessons in, including only the activities he'd stayed in beyond beginner.

Swim.

Dive.

Golf.

Ski.

Skate.

Sail.

"I would be okay never doing a single one of them ever again, except for swimming, but not on, like, a team," he told me. "Not, like, get in the pool and try to shave two seconds off your time, and that's the whole point."

I asked, "What about an instrument?"

"Like in music?"

"Yes."

"That's not how I grew up," he said. "Anyway, I didn't have time."

"I never had lessons in anything but basic school," I had to tell him, trying to make it sound like I wasn't jealous, or sorry for myself, both of which I was feeling.

He thought I had it better than he did. He was such a sentimentalist! He was about as practical as friends I had in college who majored in, like, philosophy! I always knew I'd have to be the practical half of this union.

One evening, a couple of months before I found out the news that the company was creating a new position *for me to be promoted to,* I came home from working late to find him at the kitchen table. The only light he'd turned on was the little battery-powered lamp I'd put on the counter in an outage a year ago, when we hadn't yet purchased our deluxe built-in generator. Not that we had many electrical blackouts. All our neighbors had been buying generators like we lived somewhere incredibly rural.

No dinner was cooking. No takeout had been delivered, or ordered.

Our sons were away on a school trip we should have volunteered to join as chaperones. The at-home vacation for us without them was extremely attractive, so we made a larger donation than usual to the school's alumni fund, to deal with our guilt. We were planning to stay naked and fuck and fuck and fuck, all over the house. Like we actually still had that kind of energy.

Nothing was on the table. No place settings. No mug of liquid he was drinking from, no glass or bottle either. No phone, no laptop, no tablet.

A deepness of some bleak emotion was in him. I knew at first glance he was feeling something he might have never experienced before. I was scared. But I was ready right away to jump into his down-ness, no matter how far it went—not necessarily to rescue him, but to give him some company. If he thought he was almost drowning in something awful, he didn't have to be alone. He'd done the same for me, plenty of times.

"It's not the kids," he said, first thing. "I talked to them both, half an hour ago. They're eating pizza you'd never let them have, where you'd mop off the grease first, if I bought it. They said it's epic. They want new skateboards."

"We just bought new skateboards."

"That was half a lifetime ago, in their opinion. They want newer ones. They're great. And no one we know died or anything."

I took off my coat, sat down. Waited.

The battery lamp gave off an annoying little buzz that was probably always there, but I'd never noticed it until now. I resisted the urge to get up and seize it and open a window and throw it out, and be glad if the glass part shattered. Just to relieve the awful tension.

"I don't want to go to work tomorrow," he finally said.

"Did something happen?"

"That's not it. Everything at work is the same."

"If you didn't go in, what would you do instead?"

"I don't know. Or maybe I do. Read."

"Read? Like, you want to read a book?"

"You make it sound like I'm illiterate," he said.

"Should we go out? Go to a bookstore? Is there something you want to buy?"

"It's not anything specific," he said. "I just think that what I'm doing isn't what I ought to be doing. I can't describe it very well."

"You can try."

"I already just did," he said.

My coat, which I had draped on the back of an empty chair, suddenly slipped to the floor, as if an invisible hand had pushed it. You'd think it made a racket instead of a whisper. My husband gave a startled little jump in his seat, and just like that, he snapped back to his same old self.

He looked every bit a swimmer whose dive had gone way too deep. He was surfacing. He stood up and turned on the regular lights.

He said, "Can we get rid of that lamp? I can't stand it."

"We can put it in the carton for Goodwill," I answered, because we always had a Goodwill carton going on.

"Want to go out for beer and a pizza?"

"Sure," I said.

"Then come home horny?"

"Sure."

We both went to work the next day. We were a little hungover and also pretty tired, but we managed. We kept doing that. Managing.

Twenty-six

"I found you."

As usual, she spoke lightly, airily, her voice as steady-going as an instrument only able to sound a few notes. But she didn't need more notes. She had a lovely voice, medium low and gently pleasant.

An oboe, I'd always thought. When I was in college, the first and only classical concert I went to was a chamber group playing something featuring an oboe—I didn't know what, but it didn't matter.

I hadn't known what an oboe was. After the piece ended, I had to leave. That music got to me, revealing an emptiness and keeping it full long afterward.

I'd been so unhappy. I'd been so lonely. I lucked out later in making friends, but for quite a while there was only me. No one among my fellow students grew up in a life that was anything like mine. I was a charity case in a world filled with people having no idea what it's like to outgrow shoes you have to keep wearing until after an overdue bill is paid, or to travel many miles on a bus to a dental school clinic so students will work on your teeth for free. You don't complain, because you already figured out the only important thing: your eyes had to keep looking at the future, the future, the future.

How did I know that the condition of your teeth could be the same as a mark of branding? Would label you just as indelibly? I just knew.

"You certainly didn't make it easy, Patricia," she said. "It's a good thing I'm strong and healthy for someone my age, or coming up those stairs would have done me in. My goodness, an empty plate. What did they give you to eat?"

"Salmon," I said. "What about you? Is the meal part over?"

"It is. I had the chicken pot pie."

"Was it good?"

"It was heavenly, same as always," she said.

"So was my salmon."

"Good to hear."

No one else called me Patricia. But she could call anyone anything she wanted, and get away with it.

The administrator. Here she was. The most senior of all the admins in the company. Or, as the woman who used to be our administrative assistant liked to say, with a mixture of snark and being comical, ad-*minion*. When the new regime came in, and we lost our own center in the assistant, we were bereft and mad in a way we never really got over.

But of course we went ahead and put up with having to share the senior admin with another section.

You work in a corporation, you put up with things. A rule. On an unwritten list where there is only one rule. *Put up with this.* The "this" could be anything. The rule could feel as unbreakable as if made of invisible iron.

"I'm not going back there," I said to her, doing my best to sound cordial.

"I'm not asking you to."

"How did you find where I am?"

"I know someone who works here."

"Who?"

"I'm not inclined to tell you," she said firmly, oboe-like.

Our Ghost, my team called her. She never acted snobby or hostile to us. She simply didn't disguise her preference for the other section. She was indifferently objective in all matters.

I knew nothing personal about her. The one data point I had on her was based on gossip. In a previous job, she was with a company that started out decently and became truly scummy, in a predatory sense. It was a software place for at-home computers.

They targeted people who could barely handle email or configuring a home screen. They were a "we will help you" place. They were invaders. They were grifters, covering their tracks carefully, so the grift was next to impossible to detect.

Our Ghost had been a whistleblower.

She didn't look the part: a woman close to retirement age, carefully coiffed in silver and gray, from what had to be regular trips to a beauty salon. She was well tailored and orderly, but not in a manner you'd call prim. She had a way of entering our section noiselessly and walking around as if gliding, if not outrightly floating.

Probably the reason she hadn't been let go after the takeover was that the new high-ups were afraid of her, and anyway she'd be gone soon enough.

I hadn't heard her come into the attic that wasn't really an attic, even though the floor here wasn't cushiony like at work. Yet she hadn't startled me. She'd just appeared.

I detected an underlying stress. She was gazing at me intently, getting ready to say something she was reluctant to say. I didn't have the feeling she was standing there in judgment of me. Or about to tell me, in her own way, I was an idiot for my banquet-escape. For running away from Employee of the Year. For being a rule-breaker.

I said, "How's the banquet going?"

"I didn't come to talk about the banquet. I have a message from your husband. A text."

He and she didn't know each other. They'd never met. She was a voice to him, a friendly, indulgent-to-him professional contact. He thought she sounded like an oboe, too, like the duck in *Peter and the Wolf,* which he listened to on the radio one day around the age of ten, when he was home alone in a no-school blizzard. He remembered a lot of it, although he swore he'd only heard it that one time. He still liked to hum little pieces. It seemed to me that I'd never heard him do the same piece twice, like he'd memorized it all. But he denied being able to do any such thing.

He thought my senior admin was duck-like. He didn't believe me when I swore to him she wasn't.

They had each other's numbers for times when he felt an urgent need to get in touch with me, like if a child became ill at school, or he had some question at home in the afternoon—often something he called an emergency. Where was the spatula that didn't have a rubber flat part? If a plastic tablecloth was wet on the cotton underside, and he put it in the dryer, would the plastic melt? He wasn't happy about it when I shut off communication with everyone, in order to concentrate in my cubicle. He didn't like being placed in the category of everyone.

"I can't believe he contacted you at the banquet. You've got to be kidding me," I said.

"I don't kid, as you already know. He wanted you to have the information that he saw your text about being here. He hopes you come home in a better mood than the one he expects you to come home in. And he loves you, and will continue to do so, regardless of your mood, which, in spite of his hope, is bound to be somewhat foul, and perhaps even worse than other years, at least since the change in our bosses."

"I used to like Banquet Day," I said.

"So did I."

"You had your phone on?"

"Yes. There are people in my life who require me to always be available."

"Do you have it with you now?"

"It was confiscated."

"You got caught?"

"I did."

"Was it someone in HR?"

"Correct."

"Was it the new kid? That little man-boy?"

"Man-boy," she repeated. "I like that very much, and now I'll never call him anything else. Yes, he was the one who took away my phone. I didn't feel up to arguing with him. Do you know what this office space is for?"

"Not really. Do you?"

"No," she said. "I was merely curious."

She stood erect, shoulders unslouched, head high: a not-tall woman you could swear was at least six feet. I could believe she'd come all the way up here to deliver my husband's message, but there seemed to be more to it than just that.

And here it came.

"I felt this would be as good a time as any to apologize to you," she said.

She had planned her words, more or less. She was staying on course with her regular way of speaking. Simple. Well modulated. Easy on the ears.

"You see, Patricia, with the job you applied for, and then what came of it, I was put in a very uncomfortable position."

"I don't understand," I said.

"You couldn't possibly. I don't have the option of quitting the company. It would mean I'd lose my pension, even though I haven't much time left in my employment. If I were to leave even a few days before the stipulated time, I'd be cutting off a considerable source of income."

"But why would you quit?"

"I would think it's obvious."

She gave me a moment to let her meaning sink in.

When it did, I went speechless for a moment, as if I'd never learned to talk.

"Please don't ask me," she said, "what obligations I have in my life, which I never could meet without the income of my pension. I don't mind telling you, in case you might not understand the importance, I needed to empty my retirement account a while ago. So relying on my pension became doubly important. Please don't take that as a reason to offer your sympathy."

"I don't. I wouldn't."

Then I made a guess. I would have seemed a jerk if I'd been wrong. Or maybe it would have been my turn to apologize.

"To tell you the truth," I said, "I never thought of you having a family."

"Oh, I do. And to let you know, the complaint I would have presented, if I resigned, will be given once I'm free and clear of where we work. It won't help. But still, after what happened to you, I need to speak up. For my own conscience."

"Thank you. If you don't mind my asking, do you know why I didn't get it?"

"I don't mind the question. I don't know."

"Is the guy sitting at the table with my section the guy they gave it to? I already figured out it's him, but I need to make sure."

Our Ghost didn't try to conceal her surprise.

"Yes," she answered. "I'd rather not speak about him. But I'll tell you, I plan to have as little to do with him as possible."

And that was it. She really could have been a ghost when she left me. Just vanishing. She didn't give me a chance to thank her. But I had the idea she'd know, without words.

I picked up the napkin on my table of the desk in the orange cubicle. I dabbed the lower half of my face. When I took the napkin away I noticed a few tiny greenish flakes. Cilantro. From my entrée. Maybe lodged in a corner of my mouth, or to the side, and I hadn't been aware of it. But I didn't feel embarrassed. She had that effect. *Classy.*

Twenty-seven

I couldn't remember if my children had anything scheduled after school. I wondered if I ought to feel guilty about that. But I decided, no. I'd find out what they'd been up to eventually.

Whenever one or both of them stayed for some activity, my husband couldn't stand the thought of them waiting for the late van or for some other parent who was supposed to do a car pool and didn't show up. He'd get into his car to play chauffeur. Often he'd go inside or out to a field to see what was happening.

There was not one teacher, aide, counselor, cafeteria person, maintenance person, office person, administrator, coach, or any person there he didn't know.

As for me, come time for teacher-parent meetings, my kids would make a spreadsheet of who taught what. They'd give it to me days ahead.

I would have to grade them A+, and not only for the effort. They knew their way around data, like something they inherited from me. They'd include descriptions in case I ran into a teacher in a hall. The teachers didn't wear name tags.

They'd test me. What color is the hair of Mr. Language Arts? Does Ms. Social Studies wear glasses?

I did not do well with those meetings. I never knew what to wear. Casual? Business? Lipstick?

I was an Out, inside an In-Crowd.

As if I weren't such a veteran of higher education, I would feel in every inch of myself that I was a public-school girl who grew up to be a parent paying tuition bills, a kid from *the wrong side of the tracks*. I would wonder self-consciously how much it showed. My teeth were white and straight enough, my talking grammatically correct, my knowledge of the subject matter in any given class pretty good, but then, I'd have to be careful about keeping myself from falling into the error of *knowing things*.

Like the time a teacher had hung up math tests receiving excellent grades, and I saw that he'd marked as correct an answer that was very, very wrong.

The teacher had another pair of parents to finish up with, in another part of the room. In the wait, I looked at those papers in a specific way. I was curious about the problems. I wanted to find out how quickly I could solve them in my head without seeing the answers.

My husband was whispering in my ear. Sometimes when he was back in his old school, he enjoyed being secretly sexy with me.

It could be annoying.

"I love it when you look like you're having a talk with numbers," he whispered, as I couldn't help feeling proud of myself for solving a problem more quickly than I'd expected. It involved multiplication with decimals.

"I can't wait to get home. Try to imagine why," he whispered.

Back when we were new with each other, he and I lied to our companies. We took a week off, claiming a medical procedure that needed to happen immediately (me), and a death in the family requiring travel to a distant state (him). We hid from the world in my apartment.

The first time we went to a supermarket together, during that week, he was shocked to see me checking prices before placing anything in the cart. Grocery shopping for anything besides liquor, junk food, and stuff for a cookout or party was new to him, so that was something going on too. But he was quickly impatient. He had no idea what a budget was, when the budget was highly restricted. He was the one paying, he reminded me, so would I please stop dragging this out?

At the checkout, he was, hurry up, hurry up. He had a credit card in his hand. Just before he paid, I quietly said to him the number the total would be. He knew I had not been following the scrolling prices on the cashier's screen. My eyes had been exclusively on the various goods proceeding along the belt.

The number I'd come up with was one dollar and forty-nine cents too high. That was because of a discount on something that took place at point of purchase.

He thought I was a genius.

All of a sudden he was in love with numbers.

He'd hated math the whole way through school and college! All the time in his job, he avoided direct contact with numbers!

We managed that day to put the freezer things in the freezer, the fridge stuff in the fridge, before he freed himself from his clothing, and me from mine.

So it was no surprise he was having a nice time watching me looking at those problems.

Then the wrongness of the answer jumped out at me.

No one was present in the room at this time except me, my husband, and the teacher, who had seemed to me to be a fair-minded guy. He was older than us by about ten years, a graduate of the school, and a fixture there. He didn't know I had a problem remembering previous parent conferences, or remembering him.

This was true in my general relationship with the school. It wasn't due to having a brain that's glitchy in terms of facial recognition. I wasn't trying some trick with myself to block or erase people who worked there. It just happened that many of the faces I encountered simply wouldn't register with me.

My husband felt it was normal. He told me it went on a lot—people who hadn't gone to the school ended up with spouses who were school insiders. Nine times out of ten, with faces and identities, it was total non-instant recall. No big deal!

I knew he was only saying so to make me feel comfortable with my outsiderness.

I quietly alerted the teacher about the answer. I spoke lightly, like, oh, by the way, I noticed something with those tests and I'm sure you'd want to know about it. Professional to professional, I had thought. I intended to say how great it was that kids in his classes were doing problems instead of letting calculators replace their brains. I never got to that.

I should have known what would happen.

The teacher looked at me with an expression of being unpleasantly surprised. He scrunched up his face as if he'd bitten into something unexpectedly sour. Then he carried on with whatever he'd been saying.

Afterward, my husband felt mortified. It was the first time I'd heard him use that word. He wouldn't speak to me on the way home, except to ask, "Why couldn't you keep quiet about that?"

I just couldn't. It didn't occur to me that the teacher would have a reaction other than, oops, looks like I missed one, I was tired, I was sick of grading tests, you would not believe what a slog it can be sometimes to do my job, it can numb you, thanks.

Whoever the kid was would never know the mistake! The kid would not be learning!

My husband was of the opinion that it wasn't our kid, so why the big deal?

He glared at me like the teacher did!

A few days later, having said he was sorry for being such a prick, he told me that, in our circle of acquaintances among other parents, we were permanently dropping a particular couple whose company we used to enjoy.

I'd been close, I had thought, to becoming real friends with the woman of the couple. She was a weather researcher, working part-time from her home: a specialist in predictions, glued to a screen hours at a time like I was. She made it seem that patterns of wind and currents of air were the most interesting, important things there ever were.

But she was the one who said what was said, and then her husband amplified it. How could that be? I wasn't hurt as much as I was convinced it couldn't be true. But I'd been wrong about that.

I would have liked to sit down with her and go over it: two almost-friends overcoming a touchy issue. Like a mistake had been made and we could get past it. I didn't think she had any animosity toward me, to begin with. She did not return my call to her, or my email suggesting we see each other some Saturday, or whenever. Maybe she was embarrassed she'd been found out.

My husband and I weren't the couple doing the dropping. We were the ones at the other end.

Pleasantries would continue to be exchanged. Smiles. Chatting. Waving hello across a room at some function. That was how it worked. In the weather of being parents thrown together now and then, little earthquakes shook things up, invisibly. When they did, no one talked about the tremors, the disturbances. My husband had known his whole life how to deal with this. I'd had to learn on my own about the difference between what's there on the surface of a person, so very pleasant, so congenial, and what's really underneath. Where I grew up, human weather conditions at any moment could come fully multidimensionally, as felt and seen and heard as thunder and lightning and rain.

The math teacher had not kept *my correction of him* to himself.

Together, that couple, my husband found out, and I didn't know how, had been saying I went after the teacher because the work of my own kid, typically, wasn't good enough to exhibit, and therefore I was jealous. And in addition to my envy, I flaunted my self-imposed feelings of superiority in a respected teacher's classroom, due to my arrogance, bad manners, and basic career-mom guilt, since I was *hardly ever home.*

And to top it off, they were saying about my husband, the poor man! He has to babysit their kids every day!

He was all for thinking up some type of retaliation. He had a fine time imagining what form it could take. We argued about it. We'd been married long enough that, in a fight, I became a little him; he became a little me. We switched approaches to things as if we could shape-shift.

"When they go low, we go high," I pointed out to him, feeling noble.

"Those are, as always, fantastic words, very lofty, very catchy," he said. "But give me a break with that."

His plotting ended up burning itself out. He was bummed on my behalf, now that I couldn't be friends with that woman. Maybe I'd been a little lonely among that crowd anyway.

I could feel I was the only mother with a full-time professional job. But more mothers had jobs than those who didn't. Somehow, as much as the odds might seem against it, I had gained a reputation as the only one *hardly ever home*.

It had happened that within the group of those who picked a home-based life, a contingency sprang up of women who were louder and more demonstrative.

A physician who'd left her practice said she could not understand why more women doctors with children didn't do what she did, in taking up a part-time consulting job that was perfect, because her husband, *like so many others,* came up empty in all the stuff of taking care of a child.

A former assistant professor said her PhD would still be a PhD when her kids turned eighteen, and she'd be happy to advise any academic mother to put her tenure off.

A vice president in my husband's own company said the best thing she ever did was take a huge demotion and go part-time. She had loved her career. But she didn't want to grow old with the terrible understanding that she'd been self-centered and clueless about the beautiful truth that a woman's real job is being the heart of a home, every minute of every day, as a heart is a heart in a body.

Those were her real words.

She didn't qualify her conviction. She didn't think that being a heart in a home was *her* real job. Her own personal choice.

Sometimes with those mothers I felt they had internally moved to another time zone, not in terms of hours on a clock, but in terms of decades or even a *century*.

Like this wasn't well into the twenty-first.

And I would feel that lots of people were evolving backward.

Someone who wants to stay home gets to stay home!

But. What I didn't hear, didn't see, was any such woman saying there is a choice.

And never mind all the many, many women who don't have that choice because they can't afford to be home like a heart!

It was, this is what you have to do. This is what you have to give up. This is what you have to be.

Because things work better this way.

And why would that be?

Just because!

I couldn't do the bad-mannered, obnoxious thing of walking around a gathering to ask mothers if they were Republicans, and, if they were, how far right did they lean, if they wouldn't mind saying?

The subject of politics forever came up. I was good at keeping quiet. Everyone was a Democrat. Or a self-described Independent nevertheless showing up to vote at primaries you couldn't get into unless you were a registered D. It was that kind of school.

Maybe some Democrat moms lied. Or they voted Democrat in theory and switched over in practice. I couldn't ask about that either. I couldn't ask, did you ever vote for a woman to be president, tell the truth?

"Are you a soccer mom too?"

That question was asked of me at a school-and-family barbecue by a young woman, a college student, soon to be "armed with her bachelor of arts," as she put it. I liked her. She was working for the school as an intern for their online newspaper. She was writing an article about a new club for moms. I didn't know what sort of club, but I had not been invited to join.

She and I had just met. It was clear she was not in the loop of insider information.

"Yes," I said. "Absolutely."

"You don't think the label is sort of condescending? Or something worse?"

"I think it's an interesting label," I said.

"Can I interview you?"

"Why not!"

My older son had the advantage on his brother of having known me longer. He happened to be nearby, eavesdropping. Or maybe not "happened to." I felt sure he'd gracefully, politely elbowed himself my way, probably after spotting the intern-reporter in conversation with me. I didn't need to actually see the look on his face when he started thinking, uh-oh, like he was one of his Marvel superheroes getting wind of big trouble. I knew that look.

Then you'd think he was about to throw up. He was faking getting suddenly sick very well. He thought he might have eaten something his body needed to eject! His stomach felt like a container of rolling waves, like a miniature version of the wave machine in the museum his class went to recently on a field trip!

I had to give him an imaginary gold star for being politely dramatic and also a little poetic.

Of course his brother rushed over. My second son was rarely the first to arrive at any scene, but once he did, his presence became the same as what happens when you place a magnifying glass over anything at all. He had a way of acquiring information that was almost, to his father and me, extrasensory.

What was going on? He found out in an instant. There was an even more pronounced facial expression of the uh-oh.

Mom needs to get out of here, he perceived.

And here came their father and we all went home.

I promised the son who most certainly wasn't going to puke that if he ever tried a truly epic fake-out like that with me or his dad, he'd be taken along to work with one or the other of us. We'd stash him in some corner without a single electronic device. We'd come by now and then to see how he was doing.

The threat of "take you in with me" was a powerful one.

Our kids in the last few years refused to come to days set aside for bringing your children to work. They were adamant about it. They made a resolution that, in their lives as adults, they would never connect themselves to a corporation with a dress code, or one with a takeover that made things worse for everyone working there except the people who had done the taking over. Any corporation they'd grow up to be employed in would be cool!

"Good luck with that," my husband and I would tell them.

And I'd wonder, what makes them so sure so young they'll work for a corporation?

Twenty-eight

I was still in the Rose & Emerald attic that wasn't an attic.

If I kept gazing any longer at the mountain, the sky, the clouds, all very much still there, still beautiful, still summery blue, still fluffy and white, I'd be putting myself in danger of either falling asleep or covering my face with my hands and crying, just crying and crying, like I did that afternoon at the park with the pond that only had water.

Except this time I would have to keep silent.

I liked it better when I was in a daze, like I'd been hit on the head and concussed. And I was wrapped in a cocoon of *this cannot be true.*

I also liked it better when I wanted to put a hole in the shin of that man on the shuttle.

I wondered, what else did the cheater getting my position cheat at? What cheating might he do in the future, sitting in the large cubicle with the window?

And what were his qualifications anyway, if he had any at all, if he'd ever done anything or climbed any rungs of a ladder on his own?

I wondered if I'd be better off never knowing hard, true facts about him. Probably yes.

Definitely yes.

I wondered what it was like for Turk in rehab.

I wondered why I didn't know who the old woman was. I wondered if she thought less of me for not recognizing her, not saying her name, if I'd ever known what it was.

I wondered what I might have done if people here didn't help me.

I wondered how her day was going, the girl who was the princess-prince.

I wondered if the man I bit on the raft when I was fifteen was still alive. I wondered what other girls he targeted, and entrapped. Who maybe did not have the chance to sink their teeth into his skin and afterward eat ice cream to get rid of the taste. I wondered if any girl he tried to break became broken in a way that could not be fixed. "Please, girl, or girls, or woman, or women, whoever you are, hang in there and find a way to be unbroken again," I was saying in my head, like a telepathic message I could send into the world, to float away beyond the Rose & Emerald meadows and the forest, and over the mountain, and on and on.

I wondered about my old neighborhood.

I wondered what it was like when the cranes and the bull-dozers came to knock down the rowhouse where I was a girl. If I'd known ahead of time what day it was going to be, I might have taken time off work to go and watch. Maybe.

I wondered how long it took for the rubble to be cleared away.

I wondered how long it would take for completion of the new hotel near my office park, on the new hill of trucked-in dirt. I wondered how high it would go. I wondered what their function rooms would be like, their silverware, their plates, their food. Probably their chefs would laugh at the Rose & Emerald banquet menu, would think my excellent salmon for lunch was no better in taste than if it came from a can, no better in preparation than if a cook had done the cooking in some fast-food franchise, some Burger King. Probably the hotel would get glowing, exuberant reviews for their first-class entrées, vegetables, rolls, garnishes, salads, fresh fruit picked not even a day ago in some faraway place and shipped over by a jet, and I said, softly, out loud, the only thing I could think of saying that made perfect, irrefutable sense.

"Fuck the new hotel," I said.

I stood up. I went to a window looking out at the front. I could see that up in the parking lot, the shuttles still had not been boarded and driven away.

I did not wonder what was happening downstairs at the banquet.

It occurred to me instead that a setup of office cubicles would have to be equipped with at least one restroom. You could not have whoever might work up here, or do whatever went on, trudging up and down those stairs.

I found it. At the far wall.

A closet-size bathroom. A little sink, with a soap dispenser and a wall-mounted holder for paper hand wipes. A toilet that was modern, compared to the ancient Rose & Emerald ones. When you flushed it, you didn't need to worry that what you just got rid of would come back up!

And what was this?

The sink rested on a roughly built plywood cabinet fronted with a door. I opened it.

A shelf divided the cabinet in two. The upper section, with a much smaller height, contained rolls of toilet paper. In the lower, neatly and expertly folded, were some Rose & Emerald uniforms.

Unisex, they were. Some black cotton-knit pants with covered-elastic waistbands, in different sizes, going up from largest to smallest. It was the same with the red and green bowling shirts.

Well.

I wasn't being a thief. I was borrowing.

The pants closest to my size were somewhat too big, but not too wide to fail at staying in place. I thought about rolling up the legs into cuffs, then decided on tucking the extra length into my Lost and Found ankle boots. The shirt was baggy on me but not too much. It was an overblouse, meant for looseness and comfort.

There was just enough room in there for changing out of my sweater and dress. I went practically weak all over from the welling in me of the bliss I felt about getting out of that dress. How could I have left my house in a dress so many sizes too large? How could I have grabbed it out of my closet in the first place and not even checked what was draped on my own body? How could I have been so far away from myself, so caught up in hurrying to the banquet?

Yet I'd done all those things. And the day I did those things was still this same day.

I folded up my dress into a silky packet as small as I could get it, and I opened the lid of the trash can in a corner, and threw it away. I felt guilty for being carelessly, lavishly wasteful, when I could have saved it for Goodwill. But I didn't want to be stuck with it. It wasn't as if I had a handbag as a carrier.

My sweater, I put back on, unfastened this time, so I could wear it as an open jacket.

I was transformed.

Twenty-nine

I almost didn't notice the things someone left for me while I was out of sight in the little bathroom.

The cubicle was my same orange one. I didn't need to pass it on my way to the door at the top of the shadowy stairs, but I was drawn by the new, exquisite odor of coffee.

I'd been headed for the exit so I could go—where?

I wasn't sure. My plan to depart the attic that wasn't an attic had only gotten as far as the command to myself to leave.

My lunch things had been taken away. I found in their place a fresh napkin, a spoon, a small carafe of coffee, already lightly creamed, and a Rose & Emerald logo mug, into which coffee had been poured.

And a bowl containing their most famous dessert, never offered on the banquet menu: a pudding of layered custard, chocolate, strawberry sauce, bits of almonds, and their glorious homemade whipped cream. An extra puff of whipped cream was sitting on the top, as if a piece of a cloud had glided down here from the top of the mountain.

The bowl was more like a small serving bowl than a regular dessert one. The members of my section weren't gathered around me to make jokes about my calorie intake, like, Trisha, you ever heard the saying, a moment at the lips, a lifetime on the hips? Guys! She'll have to go on a diet starting tomorrow, so we'll divvy up her portion of the weekly lunch!

A note had also been left for me, on a sheet of paper bearing the same Rose & Emerald logo: the red rose on a bright green background.

I recognized the handwriting of Our Ghost. I'd seen it often enough on the stickies she pressed to my computer screen whenever I was out of my cubicle and she needed to deliver a message from my husband.

I had a pretty good idea that when she acted as a go-between for personal communication, she was doing something exclusive to me and my husband.

After she retires, I decided, I am totally staying in touch with her.

The note said, "My phone was returned to me. The bearer of your coffee and dessert was kind enough to wait for me to write this. I felt it was necessary to let you know the search for you on the grounds has been abandoned. It's believed you are safe. Your husband is at your children's school for a soccer game. The banquet is nearly over. I'm on my way to the shuttles. I expect you won't be doing the same. But I've no doubt you'll get home with minimal trouble. I've always thought it's a good idea to believe in the saying that you never know who may surprise you. Good luck, Patricia."

I assumed that by "surprise you," she meant herself.

I folded the note into a pocket of my Rose & Emerald overblouse. I promised myself I wouldn't lose it. Then I took a long sip of the coffee, which was a little bland, but otherwise okay.

The instant it came to me that I was never going to work in my company again was the instant I spooned into my mouth the first taste of my dessert.

I wasn't immediately getting anxious about going on the job market. I wasn't asking myself any questions about my future.

I was saying, "This is really, really good."

Thirty

The banquet was ending. One shuttle bus remained in the lot for the stragglers and the sneak-into-the-bar-for-a-quick-one people, as happened every year. As soon as that one was gone, I would propel myself downstairs and find a phone.

That was now my plan. I was leaning against the idea of calling my husband to come get me. The kids would love being left home alone for what would amount to several hours on a school night— but he'd be nervous about it. He might have to round them up and practically lasso them to get them into the car. I didn't want to disrupt their routine.

Some type of taxi service would have to be available. Any place with a bar would have to know about transporting people too drunk to get behind a wheel.

So calling a taxi became the thing. I was caffeinated. I was sugared. I was feeling kind of all right in the orange cubicle.

The drawers of the file cabinet were empty. I would have liked some paper, a pen. To do what with? Maybe I could sit there mindlessly making doodles, putting labyrinths of inky squiggles all over a page, like I did at work when I was stumped by some problem and had no one to ask for ideas.

I kind of worked on my own, much of the time. I kind of was the person other teammates came to, when something seemed impossible to solve, and some executive was jumping on our internal message system to yell at us extremely impolitely, in capital letters, where the fuck is such and such report when I have to take it to a meeting in five minutes, what the fuck is wrong with you people when we pay you so goddamned much, could you take care of this thing, like right now?

Usually after such incentives to get a move on, it was time to turn everything over to me.

But one shouldn't say so, right? One shouldn't go around calling oneself the actual leader of one's team, when no one else did. One shouldn't toot one's own horn, right?

Or I could have worked in the orange cubicle on a draft of a new, updated resume.

But if I really got into it, there would go hours and hours. Darkness would fall like a lid on me and I'd be puzzling about whether or not to describe how sometimes I tinkered with a software utility because it didn't work for what I needed to do, and neither did any others I'd tried. Or I'd have to do some new programming.

Should I even say I can program, instead of sticking to data analysis? If I owned up to the whole of it, what about how many languages I could code in, and I was just starting to get involved in picking up another one?

Okay then, never mind all that. I'd be looking at a task of creating a mini-encyclopedia.

Maybe I could use this free time to draft a memo to my company. Or my department.

It could be simple. "I quit."

But I looked in the other file drawers too. All empty. It was just as well. What I really would have done would be this: fill multiple pages with words of protest.

Every obscenity I knew would be involved. I'd place obscenities together in highly inventive ways, and if I reached a peak too soon in expressing the furious inner maelstrom I intended to work up, and my words turned dull, I'd sit still awhile, on a break, and think about the guy getting the new position instead of me, completely outranking me, if I'd planned to stay on. In his new position of boss-ness, he'd be overlording me, and so I'd let that sink in and churn around, and then return to my protest, exponentially more vigorously, because what happened to me in my company was wrong, wrong, wrong.

And then of course I'd rip up the pages and put the scraps with my dress.

I remembered that a new plastic lining was in the trash can. It was pristine. No one in the bathroom before me had thrown anything away.

I went back to the bathroom. I opened the trash can. I knew I couldn't live with that guilt. You don't grow up like I did and be all right about letting a garment in excellent condition go nowhere but a dump site, never mind that the garment had cost an awful lot.

The dress was gone.

I checked the cabinet I took my new outfit from. It wasn't there.

I returned to the orange cubicle and drank some more coffee. I looked at my bowl to see if I'd finished dessert absolutely completely. I had done so. I sat there. Blankly. I started drumming my fingers on the desk, like playing along with a song I could barely hear, and did not know the words to.

Then I had company.

The old man I'd overheard outdoors saying the doorstop rock was the comet came slowly up the shadowy stairs. I heard him on every step. He was quite heavy-footed.

The sounds of him didn't alarm or worry me. I was too busy thinking, now what?

He came straight to my cubicle. He eyed me up and down.

"Hello," I said.

He gave a little grunt, standing there, catching his breath. I could tell he was chewing over in his mind the fact that I was not what he expected. Oh, my outfit! The uniform!

He asked me, "How come you're not on the job? What are you up to? We don't want no lazy heads around here, no derelictions of duty, you got that? Where's the lady I'm looking for?"

I admired him immediately. I felt that, right now, he was the only person in the world I wanted to have a conversation with.

"I don't work here. I'm the lady."

"Oh," he said. "That explains it."

He wasn't merely old. His age was probably close to mid-nineties. He was lean and lanky, with a face that was lined and weathered. I had the feeling that if someone were to call him a tough old Yankee, he would take it as the highest of compliments. His flannel shirt was a red and black plaid beneath a thickly knit-ted sweater-vest in the same shade of green as the green of the Rose & Emerald. His tan cargo pants were rumpled but clean; his boots were those of a construction worker. On his head was a baseball cap with the name of a local dealership that sold tractors, snowmobiles, four-wheelers. He wore it with the visor pulled low, like an awning which had slightly collapsed. He smelled power-fully, richly, warmly, of earth and outside air.

He slipped off his cap, revealing a crinkled dome of a forehead a few shades lighter than the rest of his sun-burnished face.

"Pleased to meet you," he said. "I got to get off my feet a min-ute, if you don't mind."

I went to the next cubicle and dragged that chair over for him. I returned to find him sitting in mine.

"You came to see me. Why?"

He looked at my feet.

"We got shoes just like them in the Lost and Found. Hell of a thing, you wearing them. Just like them. Boots, I should say. Them boots. Been there a long time. Hell of a thing to think of some lady going home from here barefoot. But, it happens, I sup-pose, along with everything else around here you wouldn't think could happen. Then it does."

"They're the same boots," I said. "I'm borrowing them."

"From the Lost and Found?"

"Yes. Why did you come see me?"

"Ah. That I don't remember. Don't worry about it. I don't mind how I can't recall things like I used to. It's normal for me these days."

"Okay. Can I ask you a question?"

He was amiable. He was open. Since he didn't say I couldn't, I went ahead with what I wanted to know. It wasn't about my dress. I'd already realized its disappearance might be a mystery to me forever.

"Will you tell me about the comet?"

"The what?"

"The rock that was holding the door open, in the hall to outside. Near the room for employees only. You didn't want the comet to be used that way."

"You work here?"

"I don't."

"Then what were you up to, down in that area?"

"I was escaping the event in Big Hall."

A connection dawned in him. "Oh that one. They got a bunch of big-shot brass in there, heads up their asses and they think the view is pretty, you know what I mean?"

"Actually, I do."

"I'll tell you, a waitress of ours, she damn near poured out a water pitcher on one of those heads, not one hour ago. That I recall. Another one took it out of her hands. Just in time. With all their bitching, those guys, they'd deserve whatever they got. I told that girl, you should've had a crock of maple syrup. That'd take care of him, if she went ahead with it. What I came for is, I came to get your tray, bring it back. No tray's here."

"I'm sorry. Whoever brought it must have decided not to leave it."

"We're low on trays. You know what else I'll tell you?"

"What?"

"Nobody that doesn't work here can know about, there's a comet on the premises."

"You mean the one that caused all the damage last winter?"

"I do mean exactly that."

"I saw the rock. It didn't look like a rock you'd see on Earth."

"You're right. But you weren't meant to see it. You know what to do? You're a nice lady. Take my advice and dig a hole in your brain. When you got it dug, throw in what you're talking about to me. Bury it, like."

"I'd rather not," I said. "I can keep a secret. You only just met me, but I can be trusted. I promise."

"Nobody's saying anything about secrets. There's no secret. Far as you know, there's no rock. Bet you don't know why someone like me keeps going around here doing any damn thing that needs doing. So I'll tell you. They don't want me to. They tell me, old man, go sit in a corner and give yourself a rest. When you're good and rested, then go ahead and croak."

"I don't think that could be true," I said.

"Believe it. But I'm not going out when I'm sitting in some corner. I'll be up on my feet. Keeling over, I'll be, like a tree that's up and had it with being stuck in one place. But I don't want no ax coming at me. Just a real fall-over, simple. Too bad there's no tray. You're a truly nice lady. Worth it, making your acquaintance."

"I feel likewise. Thank you for the compliment."

"I never saw no comet that night," he suddenly said. "In the sky. *White*. Faster than a speeding bullet like they say, with the guy in the cape that flies."

I sat up straighter, on high alert, nearly gasping out loud. "You witnessed?"

He had wound himself up, yet he spoke calmly, his voice old-man raspy, trembly.

"I did not do no witnessing."

"Okay," I said. "Maybe you forgot?"

He wasn't insulted. He grinned at me. He wore dentures, top and bottom. The clean, symmetrical, perfect-teeth whites looked splendid, not artificial. I had the feeling he was proud of them. Obviously the set had not come cheaply.

I smiled back, encouragingly.

"No trouble recalling that night," he said.

"I'd love to hear about it."

"Heart stopped right in my own damn chest. Now that would be the way to go out, like if it wasn't my heart, it'd be my own eyes. You know how eyes, they connect up with the brain? That was how bright. Almost blew out the connections. All circuits damn near shot. And I know what I'm talking about, in case you don't think so. All the fuses around here? The damn wiring? And let's not call an electrician when there's me around to take care of it? I almost fried myself up I don't know how many times. So, I *know*. And a tail was on it, big and long as a kite, but it weren't no kite. Me and her, we weren't here. Official-like."

"Her," I said. "Who would that be?"

"I ain't saying. Damn husband. You know why I ain't dead? Because I ain't going out before him. I'm dug in on that. Rooted. That's the truth."

I thought, he means the old woman. Who recognized me and knew my name. And I hadn't been able to do the same. He was mad at her for using the comet to keep that door open, while she was out to smoke a cigarette.

And then, with a great deal of groaning and huffing and mumbling, the old man heaved himself up from his sitting position. By the look on his face, it seemed that the act of telling me the words he'd just told me had already vanished from his memory.

"I wonder where the damn tray got to," he said.

I did not suggest that he carry away the objects on my tabletop. I asked him if he'd like me to accompany him down the stairs. He gave me a look as if I'd hurt his feelings, and I regretted it.

I said, "Can I see the rock? Can I touch it?"

"Nope. There's no rock."

"Okay. Can I tell you something important?"

"About the rock?"

"No. It makes me happy to know you won't be leaving this world anytime soon."

He brightened. "You and me," he said, in a tone of voice grown solemn, "may never set eyes on each other again. But when I up and go, and by that I mean, really *go*, you'll know it, same as everyone else."

It was clear he didn't mean something normal, like seeing an obituary.

"Okay. How will people know it?"

"From looking. Looking *up*."

"Like, at the sky?"

"Precisely. I got it all planned. I'm going out like the comet. Right up over that hill out there. Just like it. But in a different gear. Like in a car. Put it reverse. Trust me, when it happens, you'll know."

Then clomp, clomp, clomp went his feet down the stairs. Every step resounded, made echoes. When nothing was in the air of the staircase but silence, the space around me felt too quiet. Too suddenly lonely.

Thirty-one

The last shuttle bus was leaving. Not one of the stragglers or bar drinkers glanced over a shoulder for a farewell to the Rose & Emerald, either in sadness or good riddance, like it didn't matter that this was their last time here, that next year they'd be strolling back to the office park from the new hotel.

And why should anyone think of tipping back their head to look up at the attic, in case someone was in a window and it was me?

As the bus drew out of the lane for the turn to the main road, it faced the orchard across the way. Many trees still had their spring blossoms, and the ground was scattered with petals like feathery snow. I was too far away to see nubs of new apples forming. But I knew they were there.

Then the bus was in the road. I watched my company roll away, as if that one vehicle contained all of it: every person, office, cubicle, kitchen area, wall, flooring tile, window, desk, chair, computer, document, everything.

I wasn't bidding it goodbye. I'd only known a tiny while I'd be turning in my resignation, but my goodbye was already said and done.

I could picture myself in a standard exit interview with HR. I would give no reason why, just as, if you look at the part of your body attached to the end of your arm, you don't explain, to the person at a keyboard to fill in a form, you're gazing at your wrist, your hand, your fingers and thumb.

They would know the reason why. My leave-taking would be routine, uneventful.

Outdoors, no breezes were blowing. The clouds of dust raised by those wheels in the parking lot gently descended, then vanished. The shuttle was out of sight.

I thought of Penny Gutierrez. No one connected to my department would ever be able to see or think the words "exit interview" without a flash of remembrance of her.

She was the administrative person of my department. Formerly. The one person who gave us something to have in common, besides the source of our paychecks and where we were located in the building. And the general universe of our daily endeavors.

In that universe she was not only her own planet, she was tilting and rotating and acquiring more moons all the time. She was so good at doing her job, we believed, we *knew,* no other group in the company had it better, in terms of who sat at that desk.

Our own admin.

Or, ad-*minion,* as she put it.

When she took off early for school—she was attending a community college in the evening and some late afternoons—she did not apologize for letting a task go unfinished, or for shaking her head in a no when asked to take on something crucial, some project schedule or interdepartmental communication, like, immediately. She kept her own time sheets. Our manager never looked them over. No one supervised her.

Some of the guys called her our heart. She wasn't. Nor did she want to be. At the age of barely thirty, at what was officially a very low rung on the company's professional ladder, Penny was our own Command Central.

She gave me the right to call her Penny when to everyone else she was Ms. Gutierrez, and she was fed up, really totally fed *up,* with every single person in the company who did not make the slightest bit of effort to pronounce her name acceptably, after she'd pronounced it to them herself. I never figured out exactly when I'd come to earn "Penny." But a little while before she left the company, in fact when she was on her way to HR for what she called her *sweet loving kisses goodbye,* she stopped by my cubicle, and stood looking at me, in my doorway that didn't have a door.

This was before there was any such thing as the new position for me to apply to.

She said quietly, "Not to interrupt you, but I've been meaning to tell you, you're okay. I'm sure you have your reasons why you stay here, but honestly, and please don't think I'm sticking my nose where it doesn't belong, you don't fit in very well with these clowns."

I thanked her for her candor. I had the feeling she wanted me to go with her to HR to quit on the spot and get some goodbye love too.

Not long after the takeover, she was fired. That was when we came to have Our Ghost.

If others on Penny's particular rung had not been let go throughout the company, in what amounted to a purge, there would have been reasons to ask, why her? The purge wasn't based on a concept of last hired, first fired. I'd seen her resume because I'd participated in her performance reviews. She entered the company from a telemarketing job she was successful at, but hated. One of the original managers hired her for the data-entry pool, but she didn't stay there for long.

"Please give her a decent raise so she never wants to move to another department that might offer her more money." That was my last official comment in her file.

Within the company, below the official radar, there was an association of employees of color, with a private online platform, password-secure. Penny enlisted me to build it, as long as I only worked on it at home.

If they had a hierarchy, which she said they didn't, she would have been one of the leaders, representing all the clerical people. I knew she was a big deal in growing it and keeping it going. She kept telling me that one day she'd invite me to something, some get-together. It never happened. She arranged a gift for me of a wristband pedometer for my daily walks, which I loved, but she wouldn't let me join their club. I couldn't get into my own site once I got it up and running. Maybe later, when it matured, she'd tell me, they'd open it to let white people in, by invitation only.

A guy on my team was Black. A guy was Chinese American. A guy was Pakistani. I knew they were affiliated with that group. I'd give nudges, how's it going? Any glitches in the software? Oh, it's fine, it's intense, it's cool, we have, like, movie nights and stuff, they'd say, then go mum.

Technically, no company executive knew anything about it.

But.

A little while after the site was up and running, a high-up in the primary takeover group—in which all the members were men, and very most definitely not people of color—got it into his head to drop in and eat with us at our weekly catered lunches. We didn't invite him, nor did our manager.

Penny always attended those lunches, as a member of our team, same as the rest of us.

I'd heard that someone, not Penny, but I didn't know who, had some sort of unpleasant encounter with this man, which was never described. But people on my team started calling him I'm Not A Racist, You Are, like that was his actual name.

Quickly it was shortened to You Are, emphasis on the *You.*

You Are didn't think Penny belonged at the lunch table with us. It was pretty clear that his desire to exclude her wasn't based on her job rank, or not on that only. He was all for employees knowing their places and keeping to those places, as if glued there for forever.

It was never said. It was just there, like looking at your own hand and not telling everyone it's your hand. He never addressed Penny directly, never looked at her directly either. She grew up in New England. She was born in *Vermont*: a radiantly healthy, beige-skin, strong and solid third-generation Mexican American. As she said herself, her language skills, in everything that wasn't English, really sucked. This was after You Are asked the room at large if anyone present happened to speak Spanish.

Generally, she didn't last at a lunch the whole hour. She thought they were incredibly boring. But when You Are appeared, she stayed. We knew that she'd heard from an admin-friend in the man's own section that he'd been talking about running a review of some employees to ascertain their status, in terms of immigration. He'd made it sound like the company was about to be raided by an armed patrol ordered by Homeland Security.

That so-called review did not take place. Or I would have known about it.

Penny never outright goaded him, but she sure did love the idea of springing a news flash on him, at some point in a lunch, when his mouth was full of food. She wanted to tell him that she was an illegal alien. In those words. Just to see what he'd do.

And just to say, right afterward, that he was the one who was the alien!

One day, You Are held forth about a difficulty he was having, concerning the woodstove in his vacation house, located somewhere on Cape Cod. He might have wanted us to view him as a regular person capable of doing stupid, embarrassing things, like everyone else. He couldn't take part in any conversations about our work. He had no idea what we even did. He tended to only talk about himself.

His woodstove was a massive front-loader with a glass door. It came with the house, and it was expensive, in tip-top condition. He'd never had one before.

The first time he loaded it and shut the door, he failed to make sure no big fat log was in the way. His act of closing the door was more like slamming, unfortunately, and the glass broke, and he had to call a stove-store guy to come replace it. Okay! But then it happened again, when he was down there for Christmas. That one was just a crack. He thought it was all right to use the stove, so he didn't close it down. Smoke leaked out! A lot of smoke! He had to dismantle the alarms! The stove-store guy loved it that he got to charge double on account of the holiday. His own wife said that if he did it again, she was calling the stove guy to come over and take the thing out—and if he did it again, that would be three times, and how does it go? The famous American slogan? Three strikes and you're out! His New Year's resolution was, guess what, no more slamming! He didn't want to strike out!

No one else at the table had a vacation house. But Penny knew about woodstoves.

She said, "Does it always happen when you're getting the stove going? Like, when it's time to start a fire?"

Yes, he admitted. As a matter of fact, yes. He loved to sit watching his own fire, in a certain armchair he'd bought for that purpose. While he was packing the stove with the logs from his woodpile, he couldn't wait to settle down. He had a case of overeagerness!

Penny asked him, "Are your logs split?"

"Not all of them," he answered. "The wood guy promised to come back with an ax, and he did, but he only chopped a few. I used them up pretty quick. I'm on his case all the time to come back and finish the job."

"But why," said Penny calmly, casually, "would you place a bunch of unsplit logs in your stove right off with your paper and kindling, and leave a log or two at an angle, not horizontal?"

You could tell that everyone at the table not counting You Are thought that those were excellent questions. He rose to his feet and walked out.

The next evening, at home, I received an email at my nonwork address from Penny. She knew how to reach me that way from my work on the platform.

"A woman in the group thinks we're being spied on," she'd written. "Any ideas what to do, to find out?"

I answered that I didn't have the ability to help in that manner, but I'd get in touch with a hard-core techie I knew. I left it with Penny that she'd let me know if such help would be necessary. She never got back to me about it.

Her notice of dismissal came soon afterward. It was not a surprise to her. Every person in my section wrote her a reference. We swapped and collaborated so we'd say different things. She scooped up a new job in hardly any time, at the school where she was studying.

"I think I'll become a dean of something," she told us at her departure.

She was clear about no party, no anything—at least, not with us as a section. But we chipped in for a card with a gift card inside, and made her promise not to open it until later. Everyone was generous in contributing, even the guys who usually had to be pressured to write their names on someone's birthday card.

Her appointment in HR was supposed to last around five minutes. They made you do it in person. It was supposed to be quick, just all about taking care of the necessary forms. In HR, she joined a queue of others being let go. Into an office she went, when her turn came. She was in there *over an hour*. They only had two people working the forms. Others in the queue were told to come back the next day.

Two guys in my section went there to see what was happening, as if Penny had found herself in some kind of peril. They went up to the closed door of that office and only heard her voice faintly. She was talking as if delivering a speech. From a prepared text. But, about what?

I was never to learn details of what went on.

Around the half-hour mark of her time in there, You Are was observed going in. I heard he only stayed a short while. He was said to be a little subdued when he emerged.

And then it was Penny's last day. I was in the window of our conference room to wave bye to her.

She took it for granted I'd be waiting somewhere, ready to offer her my salute, but she made me wait a good long time before she looked for me. She was all the way to a tree by the building with Starbucks, in the last inch of space she had before I couldn't see her anymore. Other people were at other windows, on other floors, I realized. I wasn't someone she blew kisses to.

But I received a great wave, directly.

People in the company still talked about her. Still missed her.

"Get it right, and I'm not even saying please about this. It's Goo-tee-*air*-ehz, you clod."

I heard she'd said that very thing in the HR office to You Are. It might have been a little bit invented. Or maybe not. She was brave.

Thirty-two

I made it down the stairs from the attic that wasn't an attic. I was careful to mind the steepness. I was laden with the objects that had no tray: mug, coffee container, bowl, spoon, napkin.

I'd forgotten that the Rose & Emerald wasn't always open evenings. Now I knew, from the quiet, that this was an early-closing day. I would have liked going into the bar, not that I had money for a drink. Happy hour could be raucous in there. I would have liked a few moments of noise.

The patio café where I'd wanted to have my wedding reception was as silent as if those tables and chairs on their knotty, wrought-iron legs—the same ones, after all these years—were artifacts in a museum.

My in-laws were generous people.

The wedding they paid for was spectacular.

My wedding.

A once-in-a-lifetime experience, a movie production, cameras, lights.

No one was on my side of the aisle but my parents and a few people I was close to in college, still my friends—a very small group, but all of us were still okay with each other as we were, as ourselves.

The maid of honor was my husband's younger sister.

The matron of honor was his older one.

I had for bridesmaids the two women in the apartment downstairs from mine. They were a couple, both in grad school. I didn't know them well, but we teamed up to go after our landlord about problems he didn't want to fix. Sometimes, we had take-out together. They were cool about the whole thing, as in, wow, we can play at being fancy bridesmaids, and we don't have to pay for the dresses. One of them was in anthropology. The other was on her way to becoming a clinical psychologist. It was all field-work and issues of mental health to them. I predicted they'd have an excellent time, and they did. So there was that. And since my parents knew no one among the wedding guests, my neighbors left the bridal-party table to sit with them, hang out with them. "Of everyone we met, those two girls were the only ones that were normal," my mother told me later.

And there was an open bar, and a galaxy of tables center-pieced with orchids in crystal, and place settings with more items of silverware than I'd ever seen before.

The jazz band of guys in tuxedos played not one song I knew. I talked myself into dancing and dancing, with maybe half a ton of silk on my body, like I was in a costume like my downstairs neigh-bors were. But mine was a make-believe white cloud.

And there I was, getting married, moving up and up and up. *I'm so happy,* said my smile, *so happy.*

My new husband went into a mode of, *I'm not really here, and don't get mad that inside myself I'm checked out. Let's just get this thing over with.* He had one dance with me, then started downing shots of tequila, even though I'd told him he better not get drunk, and of course he got drunk. But I couldn't be mad at him.

And all along in my head, in my own private loop of a soundtrack, was the Talking Heads, *My God what have I done,* that growl-scream of an utterance.

"Once in a Lifetime," it was, over and over and over, the best song there ever was, to me, that day.

What am I doing here?

How do I work this?

What have I done?

I did what I did.

You have a life, you put up with things, you want to get ahead.

Once when I was working in my second company, I had a night out at the Rose & Emerald bar with four of the women I often ate lunch with. It was supposed to happen that we formed a group of let's-go-out-somewhere-regularly: a play, a concert, other bars, someplace for dinner where no one ever brought kids. We were all mothers.

But it was only that one time. It just didn't take off. I'd been keen about it. We went in one car and on the way I was talky. I was animated. I talked about growing up out here in this countryside, and someone had the idea we should drive by my old home.

I discouraged the impulse.

I didn't say my home wasn't there. I couldn't.

I didn't talk about my girl gang, either. By then I couldn't remember any of their faces. But voices would come back to me sometimes like pieces of old songs that are a huge deal to you when you're, say, thirteen. And the huge deal keeps growing smaller, smaller.

It wasn't that I felt ashamed. Nothing like that. I'd learned that once you tell someone you were poor, like, *poor,* and the someone you tell it to never was, you can't ever take it back. It becomes, oh, I know what you mean, one year when my dad was on unemployment, we couldn't go to our regular mall to buy clothes. We had to go to Sears!

And, Trisha, how depressing, no one would ever guess you had it rough.

And, gee, you must have seeds in you of bitterness, and that's totally understandable—as if stems were shooting up inside me, and soon I'd be filled head to toe with a personal meadow of thorny, weird, dark flowers, plus the type of weeds you cannot pull up and make tea with, or else, if you do, you'll be poisoned.

But it wouldn't be poison like the stuff in the cups of famous characters in stories and plays.

It wouldn't be fatal, not to your body.

It would be, it's too much trouble to get a book and read it.

It would be, that cow of a teacher is making us memorize a poem?

It would be, doing homework is for kids who have no life.

It would be, why wreck the fun of water by learning how to swim like a preppie asshole?

It would be, there's a rumor going around that Trisha Gilley's taking computer science with the geeks. Isn't that the best wrong gossip ever?

It would be, unbelievable! Another weird rumor! Trisha Gilley's taking *calculus*.

In the bar that night, I wondered if I'd run into one or more of my old friends. It might have been okay. Or not. I had to factor into this possibility the reality that I had basically disappeared. A long time ago. Or I had fled, like a refugee from the country that used to be my life.

The bar was packed. Our table was sticky with old spilled beer. I didn't recognize anyone. Not one familiar face of one lost friend changed from girl to woman. Not one old schoolmate. Not one old neighbor.

Or maybe I'd actually spotted someone without knowing it.

We only stayed a little while. A deflation had happened. The women I was with realized at the same time we weren't meshing together. We were trying too hard to force ourselves into a group that wasn't right for us. We were quickly very tired. It was a long ride back, on a dark, moonless night with a sky too gray for stars. It was kind of tense, kind of empty, kind of lonely.

What have I done?

It was a circle.

Here I was, in the silent, old, slightly shabby, oiled-wood foyer of the Rose & Emerald where you can take a left turn to head for the bar, but the bar was at closing time, and everything was closing. I didn't know what to do with the objects I wanted to look at fondly, as if I'd gathered some treasures: an empty mug, an empty bowl, an empty coffee carafe, a spoon with a silver oval I'd licked clean, a slightly stained napkin.

They weren't treasures. They were like props in a play. Like I stood on a stage.

I saw what I saw.

I saw *here.*

Like I was standing outside of myself, all eyes, in the muted glow of old Rose & Emerald wall lamps, in the thin bronze light of summery almost-evening, coming through windows paned with old bottle-glass.

I saw a girl in a costume at her last Halloween, dressed up as a robber, busting into that bar with a toy pistol and a bag for dollars instead of candy, and everyone in the bar gave her money.

I saw a bride, billowing in white, her hair and makeup done by expensive hired professionals who made her sit still a long time to get it all done up. While she was still, she was making a wish, like a little girl would do, to drive out to the Rose & Emerald for photographs, with the mountain and forest and meadows in the background, and then, for all of her future, she would have those photos in an album.

And perhaps there'd be a video too, perhaps of the bride strolling a foot path, among riots of wild meadow flowers, red like hearts, pink like neon, orange like sunsets, blue like the sky, white like stars, like snow in the springtime—she had pictured all that, planning and planning, can we drive out to the Rose & Emerald for pictures?

When it was almost past time to ask for the wish to come true, she covered her face, hid her face instead, hid the mouth the words would come from, feeling stupid, feeling she was teaching herself a new lesson, and it was *how to disappear.*

I saw the woman right now in a costume of a Rose & Emerald uniform taken like a robbery from a cabinet at the top of the building, which had become a place of hiding.

I'd been hiding.

Again.

I had only just wanted to hide.

Thirty-three

One evening near the end of a summer when I didn't have a bike yet, I sat on the stoop outside our front door with my parents, and a neighbor of ours came by: a man of middle age whose wife had recently left him. She hadn't been in touch with him to say where she was. The reason for their breakup, I couldn't know.

The man wasn't a friend of my parents like so many others were, among the rowhouses. But they were making an effort to be nice to him, even though I could tell they took the side of the woman, and quite possibly knew her whereabouts, which no way would they reveal.

A hard bitterness was in this man, as sharp as if every word he spoke came booby-trapped with barbs and needles.

Sometimes my mother felt moved with pity for him. Someone, she'd say, must have wiped the smile off his face a long time ago, probably when he was a boy, and he never found a way to get it back. He worked as a machine operator, the same machine every day, in a clattering, deafening maelstrom of noise that never let up until a whistle blew.

What he talked about on our stoop was the cackling buzz of the electrical wires up on their poles in our neighborhood. Was it too much to ask for in life, to have some peace and quiet in the air around his home? Did my parents know how to contact the electric company to send someone out to insulate those wires, shut the things up?

"Those are cicadas," I said.

The three grown-ups went into a little shock, especially my parents. I didn't often speak up when anyone else was around. I thought that the mistake I'd made was to say "cicadas." I'd thought everyone knew what that word meant.

"Insects," I said. "Bugs. Summer's over and it's almost night. They're right on time."

The man turned sputtery, snarly, angry. The words he let loose as he hurried away from us were too mumbled to make sense of. My mother and father were mad at me too. They wanted me to go after him and tell him I was sorry.

I didn't. I could not figure out why saying the truth was bad. The wires were silent! I suggested to my parents that they stand near a pole and listen. Then they'd know!

They didn't agree with me. A wall came between us that was never there before. It had no windows. It was solidly solid.

"If a man says something comes from electricity, then that's what is," my father told me.

My mother silently backed him up. The next time she and I were alone together, she spoke to me about what I had done, in a tone of voice she only used when something was important. When I wasn't a kid anymore, she explained, I'd understand the fact that, in life, and not just my own, but all of life everywhere, certain things just are the way they are. She didn't care one way or another about the wires or any bugs, noisy or not. But I needed to learn a lesson.

"Men. They may not always be right, but they're never wrong," my mother lessoned me.

I had no idea what she was talking about. I didn't even know how I knew about cicadas, what they are, how they never chirp when it's hot, only when it cools, how their sounds were like music to me because they meant school would be starting again; summer was ending.

Until then, I loved school.

Afterward for a long time, not so much.

There was a joke we used to tell, me and my girl gang. I'd laugh like it was the funniest thing any joke could ever be. It was about breakfast. Want to hear a good joke about breakfast? Well, you get your eggs from a chicken, your bacon from a pig, and your milk from a teacher!

When a listener looked at us blankly, it was the perfect setup for the punch line. Which we delivered with merry gusto.

Cow! Get it? Teacher equals cow?

"They're synonyms," I sometimes added, if I felt that no one would make fun of me, and it could work to make the joke even better.

I could still hear myself saying that.

Cow! Teacher! Both the same thing!

I was sent to bed early on the evening of the stoop, grounded from watching television. I knew there wouldn't be anything on that night that was any good. But it was lonely in my room. It felt vacant, like I wasn't there.

I thought hard about it all, for days afterward.

Was the real thing to be learned, never correct a man? Because it will only piss off the man the mistake belonged to? Because the man will have his feelings hurt, and the one doing the correcting, me, will be nothing but a giver of hurt? Was that what I wanted to do with my life, be a giver of hurt?

Or was the lesson about always staying quiet instead of speaking up? Because look where it gets you?

I worked it out like a problem. I was satisfied with the answer I arrived at.

It was both. It was a never and an always.

Never correct men. It hurts them. Never be a giver of hurt.

And always, always remember to never speak up.

And why would I be time-tripping like this, back to the stoop, back to the words of my mother, as I stood in the shutting-down quiet of the Rose & Emerald in clothes that weren't mine, with my hands bearing a mug, an empty coffee carafe, a bowl, a spoon, a napkin?

Because I remembered who the old woman was. The Rose & Emerald woman who knew me. Who put the comet in place as a doorstop.

I recognized her retroactively. Her old face shifted in my memory to her younger one.

"Me and her," the old man had said to me, in the attic that wasn't an attic.

The husband the attic man mentioned was the stoop man!

I remembered that, when she left the man who sat on our stoop, she didn't stay away much more than a month or so. I heard my parents discussing their reconciliation. It seemed she hadn't returned on her own. He found her, and went and got her. It seemed wherever she was, wherever she'd *fled* to, turned out to be worse than what she'd left. That was the official explanation. They moved away from the rowhouses when I was still in middle school. I'd heard she became a waitress in a bar, but nothing more.

And now I could go and find her, right here.

I could apologize for failing to know her. We could have a conversation, and surely she'd answer my questions of, will you tell me about the comet, will you bring me to where it is, can I touch it?

I could understand why they decided to hide it. The area by the door the old woman needed to keep open was an enclosure, I remembered. A small, private, walled-in outdoor place. For employees to smoke cigarettes, or whatever. When I was a girl, I thought it would be a good place to leave my bike when I was poking around, trying to find ways to sneak inside, but I couldn't get the tall, solid gate to give way to me. It didn't have an outside latch.

The old woman could lead me there!

They might have been keeping the rock in that enclosure. Or maybe somewhere in the building, in or near the private room for employees only. There might have been other rocks as well!

I realized that, in my present predicament, the most important thing of all was supposed to be *get to a phone.*

Which was still of extreme importance.

I'd simply bumped "find a phone" to the second-place slot in my priorities.

I couldn't stop thinking about the comet. I told myself I'd be careful about suggesting to anyone at the Rose & Emerald that, actually, the word to say for the rock might be "asteroid," or "meteorite." It wasn't because I'd be hesitant to let myself enter an act of correcting. Or an act of speaking up and saying the truth. I wasn't a little girl, scared of being lonely, scared of knowing about a wall without windows between me and my mother and father, and then me and basically everyone.

"Comet" was the perfect word. They had it right. Rushing from the sky, with a tail as big as a kite, but it wasn't a kite.

Thirty-four

When someone opened a side door, rich and wonderful smells of food came streaming into the enclosed, somewhat stuffy Rose & Emerald vestibule: cooked food, quite possibly in large amounts, steamed, roasted, sizzled in a frying pan, oven-baked, doughy, meaty, sweet, creamy, buttery, combined all together in such an airy rush, I went a little wobbly.

But how could this be, when they were closing?

"Ha! I didn't expect running into you. I almost thought for a minute you're new here, coming in for the training program," said the woman approaching me. "But then I got it who you are."

"Hi," I said. "The training program? Does it go on in the attic?"

"I know you were up there, but never mind about it. It's private."

The woman was about my age. Her uniform top hung very loosely on her slender frame. Unlike me, she was in clothing that showed signs of being lived in all day, being worked in. It wasn't that I saw stains. It was a general fabric exhaustion, a limpness. She had rolled up her sleeves almost to her shoulders, perhaps to show someone on the other side of the door the shape of the impressive, taut, roundly hard muscles of her upper arms. I didn't think she'd developed those arms only in the course of carrying heavy loads in a restaurant.

There couldn't have been an ounce of extra flesh on her body. Her face was as smooth as if she had a job in advertising, posing for skin-care products. A wide, flowery headband circled yellow, wavy hair pushed back off her forehead. I couldn't help noticing she had undergone dyeing that had not been handled well, or she had picked a too-artificial shade of blond, at odds with the makeup so recently, so expertly applied: perfectly pinkish lipstick, and mascara, and pinkish-blush shadow that let you look at her and not just see how tired she was, as if her weariness, perhaps every day at this time, gathered itself together in her eyes.

"I saw you in Big Hall," she was saying. "I said hi to you when you went by me, but I guess you were in too much of a hurry. So I was like, whatever. And look at you, all dressed up like us. I'll take those off your hands now."

Into a pocket of her shirt went my spoon and napkin. She took the mug and bowl to hold in one hand, the carafe in the other.

Then she said, "You don't remember me."

She spoke with the authority of stating a fact, in a voice that sounded like she'd put her words through a sieve, to remove any bits of emotion.

"It's been years, sure," she said. "But everyone tells me I haven't changed at all. It's the same old me. Like it or lump it, I always say. I'm fitter, though. Changed my color. I was a redhead a while ago but I couldn't stand it. I'll keep the blond, I think. This girl's still a pearl in a whirl, you know what I'm saying?"

She was giving me clues. Giving me the chance to arrive at the right answer on my own.

Was her name Pearl? I didn't think I'd ever known a Pearl.

I didn't know the answer.

A coldness came through me, a chill of remorse. Her gaze on me turned harder, becoming definitely unfriendly. I did what I could to run a memory-sweep, but we must have known each other long ago, in the life that stopped being my life. I came up with nothing.

I wasn't being accused of doing something terribly wrong, but that was how it felt.

"Trishy," she said. "Is that what anyone calls you, these days?"

Oh! Trishy was the me in my girl gang.

Which girl was the one who grew up to be this woman?

Nothing. It was the same as experiencing a power outage inside myself.

"I pretty much go by Trisha now," I said.

Again the side door opened. What emerged this time was a procession of Rose & Emerald staff people bearing heavily loaded trays.

There passed by us bowls of green beans and mashed potatoes, and platters of roasted chicken pre-sliced, and two large wooden bowls of salad, and two high-sided baking pans that were hot-bubbling with macaroni and cheese. And several baskets of rolls. And a large pitcher of gravy and a clear-glass bowl of fresh, vibrantly scarlet cranberry sauce, and another of a white sauce I guessed was ranch for the salads.

Dinner.

The old man from the attic took up the rear, holding a thick roll of paper towels, which I took to be fill-ins for napkins. He didn't look at me, although he walked by me so closely I could have touched him.

No one looked my way. They were heading for the employees' dining room.

One of the waiters called out cheerfully, "Hey, Muscles! Come on!"

"In a sec," answered the woman, with a wink and a toss of her head. She liked to flirt! But that was no hint. In high school everyone did, even me. Turk was not in the line. I started hoping I'd see him, as soon as the procession first appeared.

It was probably better he wasn't there. I wouldn't know how to defend myself to this woman if it came out that I'd known who he was the instant I laid eyes on him.

"I have to get rid of these things and get to dinner," she said to me. "With anyone that's late, you could end up with, like, two chicken wings and a bun, and one leaf of lettuce, and that's it."

"Can I join you? I'd so much love to."

I was making an attempt to put myself in a good light. I gestured to the clothes I was wearing, like I had the right to be one of them, because of my costume.

It was not to be. I felt I'd shown up on a stage to play a part when I wasn't in the cast. Her refusal of my request was plain to see.

"Look, Trishy, I should have known you'd be like this with me," she said. "You didn't remember one of our bartenders, and she was so good to you today. But like she and I were saying, you burned some bridges you don't want to be crossing back over. How we feel is, that's your choice. You've got the right to it."

One of the bartenders? Of course she had to mean the old woman.

"I'd like to thank her," I said.

"She only wants to have her dinner now."

"Still, I'd like to go in with you. Just for a couple of minutes. I'd be happy to get to, you know, talk."

"About what?"

"You. Please."

"Like catch up? Get me talking about, blah blah blah, my life? And the old days, walk down memory lane?"

"I really am sorry. And I have so many questions."

I thought it was unfair of her to not tell me her name, or anything solid I could grab on to. I knew that if I asked her outright, she'd go tight-lipped. Just because I couldn't place her didn't mean I'd un-remembered *hardness*.

I was looking for light in her. Maybe it was too deeply covered. Maybe I was the only one she hid it from, because I had hurt her.

"Questions!" she said with a little laugh. "You haven't changed one bit. But maybe you have. You were the one always thinking you had all the answers. The thing is, you need to be leaving. You plan to return what you're wearing?"

"I am. I will."

"It'll be better all around if you put the uniform in the mail."

"I will."

"What about the boots on your feet?"

"Those too."

"You can keep them. A swap for the heels you left under your table—real fancy, they are, like your dress. I'd introduce you to the bus boy that's bringing them home to his mother, but he's in there eating, like everyone else."

For one little moment, her tone went gentler, warmer.

"Just so you know," she said, "the lady that's getting your dress, it's a lady that'll appreciate it. She doesn't work here. But some of us waitresses, we look after her."

"I was going to ask you about my dress."

"They told me you threw it away."

"I was . . . I mean, I was . . . Well, I wasn't really going to . . ."

Sputtering, I couldn't find words to explain myself. I could see what she thought of me. I could not reveal that I'd wanted to take the dress from the trash bin so I could donate it to a charity. Who puts a garment like that in the trash? What kind of person would that be, objectively?

I had no defense.

I said, "Please change your mind and invite me to your dining room."

"I don't think so. It's just us in there. Even if I could say yes, it's a no. Your tow truck came."

"My what?"

"Your tow truck. Up in the parking lot. Did you see that guy calling me Muscles? He told me. You're all set."

"I didn't hear him say so."

"You don't work here. He sent me a signal."

"But I didn't call a tow truck."

"*Someone* did, and it's definitely about you," said the woman.

The old man emerged just then from the secret, private dining room. He ambled along in a slight shuffle. I wondered if his trip up and down the attic stairs had taken too much of a toll on him. But he seemed quite spry, and also a little tipsy. They must have been drinking some kind of booze in there.

He had an empty tray now, instead of paper towels. He was on his way to the kitchen.

He didn't come to a complete stop when the woman moved toward him. She placed the objects she'd taken from me on his tray. Then he just kept on proceeding, full of purpose, ignoring us. I wondered if everyone working here knew he planned to leave Earth as a comet in reverse.

The woman said to me, "You know what part this is, now? This is the part where people say, hey, swell to see you, keep in touch, give me a call one of these days. Ain't gonna be said. I'm not being bitchy, putting it like that. It's how it is."

"I don't think it was bitchy."

"I've been called it. Deserved it, too, half the time."

"I haven't kept in touch with anyone," I said. "I took a different direction. But you know that. Have you been working here long?"

"Trishy, don't. I'm hungry. I want my meal. No hard feelings, okay?"

I surrendered.

It wasn't as if, someday in the future, I could drag out my yearbook, my old photos, my collections of girlhood stuff: notes, trinkets of great importance at one point, a barrette, birthday cards, some pieces of junk that didn't used to be junk. I didn't have any such things. The stuff disappeared. Because that's what I did with it all. Made it disappear. I'd never felt I had a choice about that.

"Okay," I said. "No hard feelings."

Maybe she wasn't in my girl gang. Maybe she and I had never been close. A classmate. A girl from a neighborhood like mine, but not mine.

Burn bridges. It sounded like a shameful thing to do.

"Please don't ever go out," I used to say, talking to the thing inside me I once called "my own, special light."

And as the woman walked away, I was asking myself, what tow truck?

Thirty-five

My manager had a serious medical condition no one was supposed to know about. But in my department, we knew.

We never had details. Nor did we ask. He was a deeply private man, and not in a snotty or self-defensive way, but just naturally. When he came to work, his very existence was all about his job. Everything else was off-limits. He could look you in the eyes and silently let you know that you needed to pay attention to your own business, not his.

He was an even-tempered, thoughtful man, gently courteous in his everyday manners. He wasn't around our section like we were. Interdepartmental and executive meetings took up a large chunk of his time. At meetings of our own, he tended to ignore any friction, any out-of-line comments or behaviors. He could appear to have the air of a bureaucrat whose thoughts are on the next meeting, the next memo, the next progress report about him, done by a high-up who managed managers.

Maybe he felt sometimes a quiet and private despair, from knowing that what he did all day was often without any sort of meaning at all.

But he fit in. He was good at his job.

Once at a bring-your-kids-to-work day, to which my own didn't come, the daughter of a guy on the team asked our manager to describe what a manager does.

This girl was only ten, yet she had in herself an already mature core of confidence, and a well-established sense of knowing when to take things seriously, and when not to. We knew she'd been working on a project about Ruby Bridges, her hero, becoming the first kid of color to enter a white southern school. Escorted by white law enforcement officers. Surrounded by white people, in a *mob*, hating on her. Many of those people were *mothers*.

This was in New Orleans, Louisiana, on November the fourteenth, 1960, we were reminded.

This child matter-of-factly told us that in honor of probably the bravest child there ever was, she'd decided to have a hairdo like Ruby Bridges, with the same sort of bow, like in the photo that became, as she said, relishing the word, "iconic." And her own dress was similar to the one Ruby Bridges chose for that day.

"Oh my God, I thought that was only a movie," remarked a team guy, in a quiet voice our manager overheard.

There was a look from him, in that guy's direction, that was so withering, so appalled, it was amazing the guy didn't shrink at once to a pile of dried-up vegetation, right there on our expensive, soundproof floor.

The girl's father hadn't heard what that guy said. But he might not have been surprised. He and the guy were the two people who shared the cubicle that was supposed to become the office space of only one, because a move was going to happen, because my cubicle would be available *when I received my promotion.*

Anyway the father was not at that time in the good graces of his child. I didn't think it was true that he looked like a young Denzel Washington. But apparently I was alone in that. His daughter had wanted him to wear his *Remember the Titans* T-shirt. It was her favorite film so far. He had told us that the shirt was too faded and frayed. He had heavily sighed and looked away, in a private moment of feelings he didn't express. He told us, "She hasn't seen *Malcolm X* yet."

So what does a manager do?

Ours thought carefully for a moment before answering.

"A manager," he said, talking to her like she was a person, not a little kid, "has to create an orderly system for day-to-day operations."

She wanted to know, what about after the system is all in place, like, it's built?

"You have to maintain it," he said.

She bobbed her head solemnly. She got it, but, does maintaining take all day?

"No," he said. "But if anyone here, such as my bosses, really thought about that, there wouldn't need to be me."

He was hired when the takeover people had settled the new regime in place. Even when it felt past the time to stop being the new guy, he still felt new. When I'd met with him to talk about my *professional goals of advancement*, I believed he'd be on my side. When I went for the promotion, he made me feel I had a male cheerleader in him.

When I went to HR that day, and I was given the news the way I was given it, I hated my manager's guts. He should have told me the news himself.

His name was Stuart Osborne. We knew he chafed and cringed when a high-up called him Stu in front of us—or even worse, Ozzie. He kept his cool. He was chestnut-haired, with scattered specks of gray, and nattily mustached and bearded. It was probably true he kept a trimming kit in his office. He was impeccably groomed. Sometimes he wore a bow tie, so of course lots of people decided he was gay.

His wife was a potter with a studio in a former factory not far from our office park. I'd only ever seen her to wave hi to in the parking lot, on days when he didn't want anyone to know she was picking him up because he was too weak to get home on his own.

Her fingers were professionally skilled when it came to finding something on a surface that might seem like a minor blemish, but was in fact extremely bad. She had guess-diagnosed him, and made sure he proceeded to the correct place of specialty.

She did not have a health care plan of her own. She was on ours.

We knew about his condition through the roommate of one of my team's members, who had a girlfriend working in the factory-studio. We vowed secrecy.

We could be good at that sort of thing, in our team-ness.

Solid. Be there for each other.

Some of the time.

And why would it be, when I was teased, when I was set up as the brunt of a joke that wasn't really a joke, it was different from all the ha-ha-ha stuff directed at other team members?

When the other team members had something in common not pertaining to me—not that I was always walking around reminding myself I was the only woman.

But!

Why was the ha-ha-ha stuff for me always about my brain, about my thinking, about the level at which I was able to do my job?

And no one had my back?

Not even my own manager. Regardless of his commitment to maintaining his sense of decorum. Or how sick he secretly was.

And why would it be that when it came time for me to be a woman moving up to a position higher than my team's, and then I was shut down, no one talked about it?

Why would any of that be?

One wonders.

Meanwhile, in my department, our manager maybe knew we knew about his condition, and maybe not. Whatever his illness was, you would have died from it, if you'd been alive in any year up to something like half a century ago.

He didn't look sick. He looked robust. He went somewhere for treatments on weekends. He required high-cost drugs. When he entered a phase of physical weakness, it was generally near the end of a day and could seem to be plain old weariness.

The other thing we'd learned was that, in his previous company, a new health care policy was established, in which a significant portion of his medical expenses would not be covered. He must have felt it was interesting that a recruitment place, in the business of headhunting big brass, treated their own people unkindly. That was how he expressed it one day at a team lunch, in a rare moment of being a little bit open with us.

Unkindly. "That company treated its people unkindly." Like it had come as a surprise to him, like it went against everything he believed in. We had figured out that the reason he changed jobs was that he needed the best plan he could get.

I wondered if he felt relieved at the banquet when I didn't approach the table where he sat with everyone else.

The team. And also the new guy.

I wondered what he'd been thinking when Employee of the Year was going on. And then I did what I did.

Escaping the banquet!

Not coming back!

A whole new kind of banquet truant!

Disappearing!

The Employee of the Year is making everyone very nervous!

This is so unacceptable!

And also, what the fuck?

I didn't think he was telling himself I was a rude, hysterical, very badly behaved woman. He wouldn't have lost that composure of his. He was a company man.

But he was more than that. Maybe a secret smile was on his face. Maybe he was cheerleading me, in his soul.

And then it happened that I could not hate the guts of Stuart Osborne any longer.

Out I went from the Rose & Emerald, into the breezy coolness of the almost-summer evening, still not fully in twilight. I gathered my sweater closely around me. My keys were still in the inside, zippered pocket. It would not have amazed me if, in one more surprise for this day, that pocket was empty.

Dusky shadows were everywhere, soft and gray and furry. Behind me, as I made my way up the lane to the parking lot, because, *what tow truck, I have to know what's up with that, and then I'll go back inside and find a phone,* the sounds of dinner in the secret dining room came drifting to me in waves of muffled laughter, of voices rising and falling.

There was no tow truck. It had left already. It had done what it needed to do.

What I was looking at was my car. Tied with twine to the driver-side door handle was what appeared to be a tag from the towing company.

On it was written, in small, elegant script, a note. I recognized the hand of the woman who put down those words. Her beautiful bowls and vases occupied shelves in his office, different ones all the time, in earthenware colors of moss, clay, mushrooms, sand. He kept a handwritten card of hers, with her signature, propped up on a little stand.

Her note said, "Stuart knew you went into hiding. He wasn't able to reach you by phone. He always wanted to sit at the wheel of a tow truck. He wishes he could have driven that one himself. But he had to settle for me making the call. Perhaps one day you'll forgive him (and I don't mean because he didn't operate the truck)."

Thirty-six

When I was working in my first company, before I could afford an apartment, I rented a one-room place with a smell of mildew I could never get rid of, and a depressing, all-around shabbiness. But it didn't have insects, so it suited me all right. I wasn't overly bothered by the awfulness. I was too excited to be out in the world getting paid.

I was fully committed to budgeting. I knew what to do. I had a world of experience to draw from. I was a freshman in high school when I started handling my parents' finances. But they didn't call it "handling." They'd never be able to give me the credit of saying out loud how I helped them. They called it "Trisha sticking her nose in what we do with our money."

I hadn't wanted to ever again come home from school to find the electricity disconnected, or the gas. Or that a bank was hitting them with fees due to overdrafts, or another bill payment was a check that bounced, or the rent went up again, and, no, they couldn't stage a protest about it by withholding the rent altogether.

All sorts of gambling took place in the neighborhood of the rowhouses: card games, betting on horses, online poker. These were things I had no direct witnessing of. Our home was never the scene of any such activities. I only knew that cash on hand for groceries could disappear or be suddenly diminished. Or be suddenly increased, although that didn't happen often.

But there was something I had evidence of. Compared to card games, etcetera, this was big.

I couldn't stop them from spending a hefty percentage of their wages on lottery tickets. I always looked away when their disappointment for *not winning this time* filled our home with an anger and bitterness I used to think would swallow me up.

They would feel as if thieves broke in and stole everything they had. They would feel that the thing called hope was something to never have, because look what it was like when you only ever got losing numbers.

But come the next paychecks, it would begin all over again. I learned how to ration utility payments so no monthly bill was skipped and thus acquired late fees. I learned to never open the drawer where the losing tickets were stored, lots and lots of them—scratch tickets at five or ten dollars a pop, Megabucks, Lotto. Someone had told my parents to never throw those things away, for there were rumors the Lottery Commission would one day return to bygone drawings, for second chances, and the scratches might one day be good for some sort of raffle with large cash prizes.

Hope was an expense, as necessary as the rent, I learned.

And once I was out on my own, budgeting, budgeting, budgeting, I had to fight hard against my powerful urges to include *buy some hope* in my regular expenses. For a while, every shop with a counter of lottery tickets for sale was frightening to me. But I never gave in.

I knew I could never have a drawer of my own filled with losing numbers. I wasn't being admirable. I was practical. It was only out of fear, like fearing anything you could easily get addicted to.

In my crummy little rental I lived on cheap takeout dinners and whatever I could get from a nearby tiny grocery, without lottery tickets, where they sold off perishables about to go bad. And a bakery where the stuff that wasn't fresh cost almost nothing. I could sometimes get a little mournful about my circumstances. That neighborhood block was pretty rough, and might have been dangerous if a police precinct weren't right in the middle.

"Temporary." My then-favorite word. It was absolutely no doubt very, very temporary. I'd tell myself so first thing every morning, last thing every night.

On the ground floor next door to my building, there was a funky vintage clothing shop where I never bought anything to wear. The prices were low, and they also had a rack of giveaways. But I didn't have the nerve.

I'd go in and look around and realize all over again I'd never be able to go out in public in any of those clothes: paisley pants, wildly colorful blouses, hippie peasant tops, faded denim vests decorated with embroidered peace signs, hip-hugger bell-bottom jeans, polyester dresses with low v-necks and swingy skirts, suede cowgirl jackets with fringe along the sleeves.

I would remember those things in precise detail, along with the smoky sandalwood incense, the psychedelic posters, the always-changing cast of clerks who seemed to believe I was lonely, even if I showed up in there on their very first day, and they didn't know I'd politely shake my head at a suggestion to consider some really cool bead necklaces, dangly earrings, a set of turquoise loop bracelets where you wear a whole bunch of them at once.

I would remind myself I could only buy things for work. Like that was the reason I never walked out with a purchase.

But my favorite thing about that shop was not to be looked at inside.

In the storefront window, they kept for a display a large wooden dollhouse, where the rooms had miniature furniture, miniature appliances, and a family of dolls: mother, father, girl, boy, baby.

Whoever took care of the display made alterations. I never saw them being done. Usually the children were involved. It was always something weirdly out of place, and it would take a minute for your eyes to adjust, and find it.

The lid would be open on the washing machine and there would be the baby, its arms up straight in the air, as if about to be sucked into a spin cycle, while the other family members were busily doing something in other rooms. The boy would seem to be missing, like that was the different thing, unusually boring, but then, there he was, in a corner of the old-fashioned parlor, at the side of an overstuffed armchair, partly hidden and about to take to the chair the tiny steak knife placed in his hand. When you looked at the kitchen, you saw that one table setting did not have a knife.

I laughed out loud every time—laughed merrily, loudly, happily. Sometimes, after a workday, I'd realize that standing in front of the dollhouse was the only time that week I felt truly myself.

One evening, I stood there a long time. I couldn't find the new thing, and I almost went in to ask. But I kept trying.

I found it. What made it difficult was that the rooms of the dollhouse were packed with items that were changed or moved around all the time, and that went for the furniture too. The parlor might have a new lamp, the dining room a new rug, a bedroom a new bureau. On and on it would go.

What I finally saw was the girl doll, in her bedroom, by the door, which she appeared to be ready to open. She was dressed in a bright plastic Barbie-type rain slicker. It was shiny, and red like watermelon. She was clutching a little-girl purse that matched the raincoat. She was obviously on her way out. I must have looked in the direction of that doll six or seven times before I noticed she did not have her head on. There was only a knobby screw protruding from the top of the torso. I thought the head was nowhere to be seen, until I finally made it out, in the midst of the stuffed toys that were always nicely arranged on her always nicely made bed, with its four posters and white chenille spread. There was a tiny teddy bear, a tiny panda, a tiny cat, and the head.

I came close to wetting my pants, I laughed so hard.

The clerk that day was someone not new. She came out to the sidewalk. She probably had only stopped being a teenager a little while ago, and she didn't wear clothes of the shop like the others did. In fact she dressed similarly to me, like she had a nine-to-five job somewhere and this was her fun second gig.

She might have been the creator of the alterations. I liked to think so. I asked, but she said it had to be kept anonymous.

"I bet you think that's the best one ever," she said.

I told her she was right. I loved it.

And she said, "You're so brave."

She didn't say why she thought so. She wasn't a clerk who ever encouraged me to buy something. We'd never had a conversation before, not counting hi and bye. Our words that day were the only ones we spoke to each other. She said what she wanted to say, and went back inside.

And that was what was going on in my head during my drive home from Banquet Day.

I still knew those countryside roads, their curves, their narrow stretches, their sudden ups and downs in tiny hills. I looked at no houses. I loved the miles where there weren't any streetlights, the feel of being alone in the dark, hardly any other cars around. I had no fear. In my head, I was back at the shop. I hadn't thought about that place in I didn't know how many years. Maybe this was the first time I knew I hadn't forgotten it.

Thirty-seven

My sweater was buttoned up, but you'd think I came home every evening in a Rose & Emerald uniform. That was the reaction I received. From my sons. In the kitchen. Sitting at the table doing nothing. No phones, no hand-held game devices, no tablets. The table was bare, pristine.

No sounds but the quiet thrumming whoosh of the dishwasher.

The sink was empty, the counters clean and orderly. The dish towels were neatly placed on their hooks, the pot holders on theirs. No traces were on the floor of anything spilled, dropped, or brought inside on the bottom of someone's feet.

Dad was asleep? On the couch in the living room? He said he'd get a book to read, but he was too tired? He lay down and zonked out, and they took off his shoes and put a blanket on him?

Was that why they were so quiet, so they wouldn't wake Dad, considering how early he got up, crack of dawn and he was on his feet rushing, every day?

Mom, no. Dad could sleep through anything. You could put buds in his ears and turn up a song really loud and he'd be, nothing, like a corpse or something.

Did you put buds in his ears?

Only one second and it wasn't that loud of a song.

My kids. Obviously something was going on. They were shaken. I didn't need to activate the invisible, inner-body, organic device that begins to shape up around the time you're so pregnant, you waddle around and pee every fifteen minutes, and you're mad at human evolution. Why can't a baby crawl out of a belly pouch like a marsupial such as a kangaroo, wallaby, koala, opossum?

But thanks to the device, which you're also pregnant with, and maybe that accounts for the extra aches and pains you have in places you never had aches and pains before, you have a ready way to get to the bottom of whatever is secretly disturbing your kids, when they've been geniuses at keeping the disturbance deep-down hidden. And meanwhile, on the surface, they're just their same old selves.

Last summer, my kids came home from their day camp appearing fine in every way. My device was dormant, but I started getting warnings, in very annoying little blips, smack in my center, like the dull throb of an old injury that acts up now and then. The message the device sent me was, activate, activate, activate.

It can be an ordeal. You can slog through hours and hours of getting nowhere.

Finally it came out that a boy was attending the camp as a visitor. He was spending the summer with relatives, and lived somewhere in the middle of America. It was his first time in New England. He was the age of my younger son, then nine.

One day they were sitting around with a staff member who was a teacher and a woman. The kids were talking about places they'd like to go for an upcoming field trip that hadn't been organized yet. The visiting kid said he wanted to see battlefields of the Civil War.

He was a history buff, he explained. It was his favorite subject. He'd already shared the information that he was always at the top of his classes—all the best grades were always his.

The teacher suggested that he must have meant the American Revolution, not the Civil War. In Massachusetts, she calmly and gently let him know, there were lots of Revolution places, for example in Boston, Cambridge, Lexington, and Concord. The regular kids in the camp were Massachusetts kids who'd toured and studied those places already, but maybe it would be nice to have a trip to Boston, say, to walk the Freedom Trail again.

Battles of the Civil War, the teacher pointed out, did not take place anywhere nearby.

And here came the trouble, told by my younger son to his brother, who was the one to brood and brood about it, to the point where I practically had to pull it out of him with an invisible excavator, digging and digging and digging. My husband tried to help at that stage, but the job of excavating was mine.

Our younger son had no problem with what happened. The visiting kid was an asshole, Mom and Dad, sorry to use that word, but it's the only one that's right.

When the teacher finished her explanation, the visiting kid told her that she was way out of line, and he would no longer take part in any group she was running.

Soon afterward, his father turned up at the day camp, as he was visiting the relatives too. He found the teacher running a group about looking in microscopes at insects, which was so awesome to my younger son, he almost missed what the father said to the teacher.

Which was this: he, the father, had worked out an arrangement with the regular school of his son, so that no female teacher spoke a correction to him—not in front of others, and not privately. The father wanted the agreement honored at the day camp. If someone who wasn't a man needed to correct his son, that person, that woman, would have to bring the correction to a male, who would then take care of it.

The father was telling the day camp teacher his son had done the right thing by telling her that, indeed, she was out of line, way out of line, in not bringing to a male the issue of which battles occurred in Massachusetts, and which didn't. The day camp teacher had violated his son's right to never go through the hassle of dealing with a woman who was out to get the better of him by making him feel he was weak, dumb, and humiliated.

The day camp had to choose between the teacher and the kid. They threw the kid out and told him, never return.

My older son's torment was that he thought the father had a good point. He was always hearing stuff about how the worst thing that could happen to boys in a school is to have a female principal, the worst thing for a man in a job is a female boss, the worst thing for our country would be a female in the Oval Office.

It couldn't possibly be right to let the worst things happen.

Maybe it makes everything work better if you stick with, like, that belief.

Even if you don't have that actual belief yourself.

Like, if your family's Democrats, then you are too, like you inherit it, and anyway, Democrats are cooler. That's how he'll vote when he's old enough to start voting, which he already knew he would do, or else his parents would get after him and also be disappointed. But he might lie about it. Nobody can know how someone else voted. He might vote for whoever had the belief of the father and the son. Like it was his duty, being a guy.

Well then.

My husband and I went at it jointly. First it was Mom and the boy alone, then Dad and the boy, then the boy and the two of us, then all of us. It took days and days, talking and talking and talking, and we grown-ups, at least, were afterward completely wiped out.

Our younger son had let us know that the only problem his brother had faced was the temporary loss of his ability to know when someone is an asshole.

So now, fortunately, on the evening of Banquet Day, I could go on alert about my kids simply by looking around.

Something was hidden, but it was on the verge of popping out. One way or another. I wouldn't have to probe hard.

The shaken-ness was in their stillness. The clean kitchen. The quiet. I decided then and there that cleaning up after meals would no longer be something I was willing to do on my own—I could not believe I'd put up with that for so long! But for now, that could wait.

Whatever this was, it was not a minor issue. Something at the center of everything in their lives wasn't doing a good job of being the center.

Mom walking through the door, just that, Mom coming home today did not throw around them thick, warm blankets of, here I am, here we all are, look, everything's normal, everything's solid.

They'd eaten all the dinner. Burgers and fries. And that broccoli that isn't disgusting, because it comes all cheesy and it doesn't have those green tree trunks, just the tops, chopped up, and Dad put some hot sauce in, and why would they save some dinner for me when I had a big lunch *at the banquet?*

Which they expected I'd still be full from. In fact, they'd known their whole lives I didn't like broccoli frozen in the freezer in a container for the microwave. Dad did though. I was always on their and Dad's backs about how cheese in a sauce from a factory is crap and totally fake.

If I ate cheese *at the banquet,* which they didn't know about, all day, until they got together with Dad and he told them, then the cheese I might have eaten, not that they cared what I ate, in a restaurant, in a *banquet room,* wouldn't be fake from a freezer, and I must have approved of it, must have liked it, sitting there at the banquet *they didn't know I was at.*

All day.

A whole, whole day.

In school.

Just like it was any regular day, Mom's at work, same as it ever was.

And so there they were, all the whole day, going to classes and stuff *not knowing where their mother was.*

That is, they were believing, *truly believing,* Mom was somewhere she wasn't.

Would I stop and think about that please, would I understand it was *not okay* to believe that I was at work, and I wasn't?

It's like, you know, on a clock when it's daylight savings day, not like on phones or anything electronic where it changes automatically, but on the wall clocks, where you have to do it yourself, and also in the cars? If you didn't know it was daylight savings day, like you didn't look at the time on your phone, you have to find out the truth later on, and it will completely *screw you up*.

And a compass.

So there's North the needle points to, like, always. It doesn't do anything else. Unless!

If you're south of the *equator*, it isn't North. It's South. The needle has to point to *South*.

Of all basic things, points on a compass are in, like, the top ten most basic things ever. They can't be messed with. So what happens if a kid is north of the equator, *which we are, which we always have been*, and the kid looks at a compass and the equator is like five hundred thousand miles away, but the needle says South and the needle cannot tell a lie, *magnetically*?

It makes the kid believe he got turned upside down, Mom, literally.

Like the *globe* got turned over.

Okay! And this is because, guys, can I have a minute here? What you're telling me is, I was somewhere, and that's what you thought, same as always, Mom went out the door today, so Mom is somewhere. Am I getting that right? But I was at a different somewhere?

Yeah.

Yeah.

And I'm Mom, so I'm time on a clock and what the compass has to say?

Kind of.

Yeah, sort of.

And you do all that with the clock and the compass and you're my same two kids who believed, please remember this with me, since you both did it, you couldn't memorize the capitals of all the states, all at once, when there's only fifty capitals, and you wouldn't even try, like you felt you didn't have the mental capacity for it? Like you don't have much going on up there, either of you, by way of a brain?

Mom, no fair.

Don't be going off track, Mom.

So tell me what is this really about. You and me, *we go back.* I know it's not about, you didn't know where I was. For that you would not clean up after dinner. I bet Dad didn't make you. I bet he zonked out before you put one single plate in the dishwasher.

We rinsed them first. In case you're wondering.

With the sink sprayer?

Yeah.

And you didn't squirt each other? You're both dry.

We didn't.

We're out of dishwasher detergent, Mom. We almost used the one for the washing machine, but we had enough.

Okay, that's great. So let's not keep going with the somewhere you thought I was. I'm not still full. I'm starving. I'm making something to eat. You want something?

I could eat.

I could eat too. Dinner wasn't that good. We only had seven fries each. Dad didn't have any. Only fourteen were in the bag.

We're out of ketchup, Mom.

Fine. Good. Here I am, sitting down. Before I fix us something. What the *hell* is up?

"They think we're getting a divorce," said my husband, coming into the kitchen. "They think you've been acting strange, so they figured out you want to divorce me. But you decided we shouldn't tell them until after we hire the lawyers."

"Guys, is that for real?"

Our children seemed to have run out of words, as batteries run out of juice. I had to put them out of their misery right away.

"How was I acting strange?"

The older one went tight-lipped, rolled his eyes, shrugged his shoulders.

His brother did exactly the same.

"Your father and I are not divorcing. You were very creative, but you figured it wrong. You know what that means? It means you get a zero. For a flunk."

"That's what I told them, although not in those words."

My husband. He was rumpled, sleepy, stubbly in chin and cheeks. He was still in his work clothes, minus his tie and jacket. He was a year older than me, but suddenly he looked like he was aging a lot faster than I was.

Darkish half circles were under his eyes.

There were circles.

Joni, I thought.

Because the first time he and I were together in a car with the radio on scan, we both moved to hit it to play that song. A good song hadn't come on for what felt like a long time, not even on the oldies stations. What did we have in common anyway, the two of us? It had seemed that getting together was not the best idea either of us ever had.

Go round and round and round in the circle game.

He told me that everyone's supposed to think the version by Judy Collins was better, owing to the fact that she was loved, and lots of people thought Joni was weird. But the Judy Collins one sucked.

I'd been just about to say the same thing. I wouldn't have thought he even knew who Joni and Judy were.

You drag your feet to slow the circles down.

"Hi," I said to him.

"Hi. I heard you talking about food. Woke me up. I could eat too. What are you making?"

"I don't know yet. Maybe you could come up with something?"

"Okay, sure."

I stood up to go to him. At the same time, mindlessly, I reached for the top button on my sweater, then the second, third, fourth.

I still had that desire to remove at least some of my clothing every time we'd been away from each other, and then we were back.

He said, "What are you *wearing*?"

"It's a long story," I answered.

Thirty-eight

You were supposed to give tangible, straightforward, information-only answers during an interview with the robot.

My earlier meetings with actual people had gone about as well as I'd hoped. In terms of the part where being on the job market is like going on a date with a stranger, I was open to a second encounter, a third, a fourth. And so, somehow, were they.

Not that I wasn't nervous. Holding your future in your hands is fully and profoundly exhausting when you're not young anymore, not cushioned in cluelessness about reality. It's a generator of anxiety. It's definitely no fun.

Here is my future, and I'm not having an easy time keeping it safe, you're saying, as if everything ahead for you is as heavy in the bowl of your hands as a ball made of iron. It keeps getting bigger like it's alive. You have to deal with your desire to drop it, or do a shot-put thing and heave it against something that will break, that can never be repaired. You might have the fear that, in causing some wreckage, you can make yourself happy.

So I was going through some ups and downs.

This place had no HR. The person taking care of the business of employees was a juggler tossing balls of other responsibilities in the air, and it was no big deal, I was told, because plenty of people here had multiple jobs, and nothing was ever boring. I would have an office. A room of my own. With walls and windows and a door I could close whenever I wanted, although I doubted that would be often. I might want to keep it open in case a robot walked by.

There were quite a few. I wanted to know them all.

Yet I was afraid of getting my hopes up to a point where a crash-down might be something I couldn't quickly stand up from, walk away from. I was scared of being flattened.

I was scared, period.

Because hope can be a dangerous thing.

Everyone knew that the only reason I'd been asked to come in, in the first place, was due to a hard-core tech woman who was one of my roommates in college. We rarely saw each other in person, but we both loved our long rambling video talks, late on weekend nights, while our husbands and kids were sleeping and we each had a bottle of wine. We were committed to being friends for life. She had told me not to worry about my future. She knew some senior engineers she wanted to speak to about me. So she made some phone calls on my behalf, in a "give my friend a chance" type of way.

I couldn't help feeling a little like I was a charity case.

And I had no idea what she told them about me. She didn't always keep to lines separating what was personal from what was exclusively your job. I knew that in her own workplace, everyone knew everything about everyone. She might have shared the information that my kids were freaking out, hopefully temporarily, but freaking out all the same. Or that my husband wanted to either switch to something part-time, or be a Dad Staying Home for the next bunch of years, God help him, as my friend had put it, and of course there'd be no pressure on the primary wage earner, me, willing to take a pay cut, which I'd basically have to do, wherever I went that wasn't anything like where I'd been.

Then they contacted me so they could send me to this robot.

I was alone with it in a comfortable small room quietly tucked near the top of an old brick building, which long ago had been a grammar school. There were bright, homey curtains on the windows, walls of soundproof tiles, a shaggy rug, and a very old wooden desk and chair obviously once for a teacher.

The robot sat on the desk. It was small enough for someone strong to pick up and carry, but large enough to be imposing. It had not been designed to look human in any way.

At first, I did the very human thing of attempting to see a face with at least a pair of eyes, in the random-looking assortment of knobs, cylinders, tubes, little wheels resembling fat tires, and all sorts of circles, like polka dots in different sizes, lighting up and gently blinking. It was gleaming with silver and shiny with obsidian black. It looked like a state-of-the-art, highly sophisticated, professional espresso machine, which no one had finished off with a means to deliver liquid.

I found it disappointing.

I'd wanted a reminder of *Star Wars*, like I'd meet and greet a cheery, adorable descendant of R2-D2 or C-3PO. My husband was voting for a humanoid-android he'd get to visit when he came to see me at work, *if I got the job*, which he was vigorously confident about.

My kids hoped hard for a cool new version of the Marvel genius-supervillain Ultron. They had fantasies of me sitting down with a machine equipped with so many ways to harm and kill, or seize control of a human mind, I'd come home with the announcement I was abandoning this possibility, having been so terrified, I'd never go back, and then *you and Dad won't sell the house and make us move somewhere sucky and have a different school, which no way will we actually go to, and what do you even know about robots, Mom?*

Analytics are analytics. Code is code. Data is data. I do what I do.

That was what I said to the robot by way of not directly answering a question about my previous experience, and how it applied to the job I was seeking.

In doing so, I felt the same shiver of that dumb glee I created for myself now and then in my car when the GPS told me to proceed ahead through an intersection, and I'd take a turn instead, just to do it. To see what would happen. To not just blindly obey. I never thought that this was absurd of me. It felt necessary.

But maybe that would never happen again. Maybe that sort of thing was only an act of protest carried out by the version of me who was corporate.

I was sort of a refugee now. Hoping this whole other country would let me in.

And I was fucking it up!

And I couldn't help it.

I'd already told the robot why I left my previous job. I laid out the biggest-deal things. They had chosen me Employee of the Year, but I didn't want to take up time explaining why it was such an offense, such an abomination. Members of my team made jokes about my brain when I solved a problem they couldn't, and those jokes came loaded with daggers. If I'd stayed there, I'd have to look in a mirror every day and know I was looking at a coward. And I had reached a point where I was completely ready to not be corporate, although frankly, I was having a hard time of it. But I was working on a program in my head to deprogram myself, while doing my best to be optimistic.

This wasn't a lie detector test. Yet I had the feeling the robot would know I was telling the truth. Words were simply coming out of me how they wanted to come out.

The voice of the robot was smoothly pleasant and soothingly neutral, like calling the service desk of your car-repair place, and there's a new someone taking your information. You can't tell if the someone is male or female. They just want to be nice to you so that, when their company sends you a survey for your opinion of the interaction, you'll hopefully be nice to them back.

The robot was patient, consistent. All my answers were accepted equally, with responses of affirmation, like, okay, got that, let's move along now, shall we?

Until.

"Data," said the robot, repeating a word of mine for the first time, as a circle of light beamed on. It was one of the larger polka dots, and had not lit up until now.

"Would that be," said the robot, "Lieutenant Commander Data, of *Star Trek: The Next Generation,* and also of films, most notably *Star Trek: Nemesis,* in which it's up to him to save the Federation, and also his captain, not for the first time?"

I saw that I just had to roll with it.

If I ended up failing in this particular quest, it couldn't be about me not knowing this stuff. My kids were able to reel off names of *Star Trek* characters when they could barely count to ten or say the alphabet. When my husband greeted me at home with the news that his day had been a bad one, I would know immediately how bad, depending on which species he felt he'd been out there fighting. If he said Romulans, I'd be mildly concerned. If he said Borg, or Dominion, it was best if he went to bed extra early, with maybe a large gin and tonic.

"Yes, the Lieutenant Commander, of the *U.S.S. Enterprise,*" I answered the robot. "You're exactly right. I'm very impressed."

"Thank you. May I ask you a question which does not require a response?"

"Please do! I'll respond, if I can."

"Who is your favorite of the captains?"

I didn't hesitate. "Sisko," I said.

"I see. That's fascinating. Many people choose Picard. Please explain your choice."

"Well, for one thing, Sisko has a god for a mother. He's got that going for him."

There was a silence. I wondered if the robot was getting tired and needed a nap. Or if it was starting to lose interest in me. I did not feel weird for believing it had a whole inner world of thoughts, complications, states of mind. I was talking to a mind.

I might have been falling a little bit in love with the robot. I felt terrible for being so disappointed at the moment we first met. Suddenly I realized that, sitting there, in the chair of a long-gone teacher, I was having a really good time.

"A god for a mother," repeated the robot.

Then, after a small pause, it said, "The Trojan hero Aeneas also had such a mother, by the name of Venus, known to the Greeks as Aphrodite. Aeneas had that going for him too."

I could have sworn the robot emitted a sound of chuckling, like it was finding its own self quite clever. I remembered, in a warm flash of pleasure, what it was like for me to be a kid in my room, opening a heavy, lavishly illustrated, encyclopedia-like book I'd discovered at a yard sale in someone's garage, where I'd gone with my parents to see if we could find some clothes for me. A girl of that family went to my school. She was about my size. Until that book came into my hands, I wanted to shrink myself into a tiny ball of nothingness, and disappear.

The title, I didn't remember. Something about Greek and Roman mythology for children. Turning those pages, dazzled, enraptured, I felt I could not have cared less what clothing I wore to school, or if I even wore clothing at all.

Then the robot had another question for me I did not have to answer.

"Which creator of epic works in the classical period do you prefer of the following two: Homer of ancient Greece, or Virgil of ancient Rome?"

"Virgil," I said. "No contest. Odysseus, for example, in my opinion, is a prick."

Another silence.

Uh-oh, I thought. I hadn't meant to say that. Did I need to apologize?

But the robot beat me to the next thing spoken.

"Would that be, what occurs when a sharply pointed object, such as a needle or a nail, causes a small puncture?"

"Not exactly," I had to say.

The interview was over. There were no sounds in the shutting down of the robot. It was as quiet as humans closing their eyes to go to sleep. When the lights went dark, I realized how much it bothered me that I didn't have the chance for the next thing I'd hoped to talk about.

The comet. I'd wanted to touch the Rose & Emerald rock. I had stuck before with the explanation to myself that I didn't know why I felt so compelled to be in contact with it.

The truth was, for a little while on Banquet Day, I believed my luck would change if I held the rock in my hands. A magical thing might have happened. Instead of staying away from my team at their table, I'd join them, because the cheater-guy they gave my position to had disappeared. He had just simply vanished, as if vaporized.

I'd be there in his place. Many apologies from high-ups would come my way, about the mistake that was made in passing me over, in *shafting* me. If the cheater somehow rematerialized, they could give Employee of the Year to him instead of me. I'd clap and clap as he went around Big Hall, shaking hands with executives and getting pats on the back.

But I would soon have a chance to discuss the comet with my new friend.

I had a new job!

Acknowledgments

I'm grateful and thankful for everyone at Coffee House Press for giving books of mine a home, along with cheers and love for my characters.

Thank you, Chris Fischbach, for being there for me all these years, as a wise, trusted publishing guy and dear friend.

Thank you, Lizzie Davis and Carla Valadez, my collaborators, for your talents and skills in editing this book so carefully, warmly, and gracefully.

And to Philippa Brewster, first reader of my manuscripts, in the roughest of drafts and again and again through revisions, for my whole lifetime as an author: thank you for the gifts you brought to my work, and for your faith in me, and your constant eagerness to enter the worlds of my novels, like a traveler with a suitcase always packed.

Coffee House Press began as a small letterpress operation in 1972 and has grown into an internationally renowned nonprofit publisher of literary fiction, essay, poetry, and other work that doesn't fit neatly into genre categories.

Coffee House is both a publisher and an arts organization. Through our *Books in Action* program and publications, we've become interdisciplinary collaborators and incubators for new work and audience experiences. Our vision for the future is one where a publisher is a catalyst and connector.

LITERATURE
is not the same thing as
PUBLISHING

Funder Acknowledgments

Coffee House Press is an internationally renowned independent book publisher and arts nonprofit based in Minneapolis, MN; through its literary publications and *Books in Action* program, Coffee House acts as a catalyst and connector—between authors and readers, ideas and resources, creativity and community, inspiration and action.

Coffee House Press books are made possible through the generous support of grants and donations from corporations, state and federal grant programs, family foundations, and the many individuals who believe in the transformational power of literature. This activity is made possible by the voters of Minnesota through a Minnesota State Arts Board Operating Support grant, thanks to the legislative appropriation from the Arts and Cultural Heritage Fund. Coffee House also receives major operating support from the Amazon Literary Partnership, Jerome Foundation, Literary Arts Emergency Fund, McKnight Foundation, and the National Endowment for the Arts (NEA). To find out more about how NEA grants impact individuals and communities, visit www.arts.gov.

Coffee House Press receives additional support from Bookmobile; Dorsey & Whitney LLP; Elmer L. & Eleanor J. Andersen Foundation; the Matching Grant Program Fund of the Minneapolis Foundation; Mr. Pancks' Fund in memory of Graham Kimpton; the Schwab Charitable Fund; and the U.S. Bank Foundation.

The Publisher's Circle of Coffee House Press

Publisher's Circle members make significant contributions to Coffee House Press's annual giving campaign. Understanding that a strong financial base is necessary for the press to meet the challenges and opportunities that arise each year, this group plays a crucial part in the success of Coffee House's mission.

Recent Publisher's Circle members include many anonymous donors, Patricia A. Beithon, Anitra Budd, Andrew Brantingham, Kelli & Dave Cloutier, Mary Ebert & Paul Stembler, Kamilah Foreman, Jocelyn Hale & Glenn Miller Charitable Fund of the Minneapolis Foundation, the Rehael Fund-Roger Hale/Nor Hall of the Minneapolis Foundation, Randy Hartten & Ron Lotz, Dylan Hicks & Nina Hale, William Hardacker, Kenneth & Susan Kahn, the Kenneth Koch Literary Estate, Cinda Kornblum, Jennifer Kwon Dobbs & Stefan Liess, the Lenfestey Family Foundation, Sarah Lutman & Rob Rudolph, the Carol & Aaron Mack Charitable Fund of the Minneapolis Foundation, Gillian McCain, Mary & Malcolm McDermid, Daniel N. Smith III & Maureen Millea Smith, Enrique & Jennifer Olivarez, Robin Preble, Nan G. Swid, Grant Wood, and Margaret Wurtele.

For more information about the Publisher's Circle and other ways to support Coffee House Press books, authors, and activities, please visit www.coffeehousepress.org/pages/donate or contact us at info@coffeehousepress.org.

Ellen Cooney is the author of ten previous novels, most recently *One Night Two Souls Went Walking*. Her stories have appeared in *The New Yorker, Ontario Review, The Literary Review,* and many other journals, and have been listed several times in *Best American Short Stories*. She has received fellowships from the National Endowment for the Arts and the Massachusetts Artists Foundation, and has taught creative writing at Boston College, the Harvard Extension School, and MIT. A native of Massachusetts, she lives on the Phippsburg Peninsula in midcoast Maine.

A Cowardly Woman No More was designed by
Bookmobile Design & Digital Publisher Services.
Text is set in Adobe Caslon Pro.